BOOKED
FOR
DEATH

BOOKED FOR DEATH

Miriam Borgenicht

St. Martin's Press
New York

Library of Congress Cataloging-in-Publication Data

Borgenicht, Miriam.
    Booked for death.

    I. Title.
PS3552.075B6 1987   813'.54   87–16361
ISBN 0–312–01106–7

First Edition

10 9 8 7 6 5 4 3 2 1

BOOKED
FOR
DEATH

1

EVERYBODY FEELS KINDLY toward one betrayed by love. Let a woman get rejected by a man and she's an instant object of fond concern. Friends suddenly realize she was too good for him. Acquaintances wonder how a girl so attractive could have fallen for that boor. Business associates resolve to be more solicitous of her in future. And all of them feel the urge to be on the lookout for a man who will give her the love and solace she obviously deserves. Condescension masquerading comfortably as good will.

But if the rejection goes the other way, if the woman, that is, decides she has made a mistake, a cold reception awaits her. Still worse if she decides it a week before the wedding. And infinitely worse, horrendous, if the man in question is one for whom everyone has reason to feel a certain amount of respectful sympathy. Finally, let the man be found dead of what seems to be a self-inflicted bullet wound the day following his heartbreak, and the woman is an outcast, a pariah, an embarrassment to all who know her. Why for so long did they consider her sweet, charming, bright, competent, appealing?

Actually, it was ten days before the wedding when Celia Sommerville told George Theroux she couldn't marry him. And there was no long period of deliberation, no time when she weighed pros and cons, George's splendid academic standing against his rigid attitudes, his decency against his humorlessness, his solid respectability against his unimpressive looks. In fact, when they met for dinner on the crucial night, she looked forward to an evening like any other. Good though carefully not expensive dinner, talk focusing mainly on George's classes, lovemaking in her apartment where the bed was rather too narrow, coffee and a snack for George before he went home well before midnight because when a man was fifty-five, as he often remarked, he needed a good night's sleep. Once she said, Oh, George, be a sport and stay all night, but he shook his head and said he couldn't get a handle on the day unless he woke to his customary routine.

After they were married, of course, the customary routine would take place in the pleasant apartment they had settled on. Pleasant but decidedly not their dream house. Not George's, at any rate. For him, this was a house north of Boston, 37½ precisely measured minutes from the university where both of them worked. But after countless visits to the house and considerable walking in the acreage that surrounded it, he said with real regret it was no go. You had to keep a handle on expenses. It was not true that two could live as cheaply as one. Marriage was a state in which those things one had regarded as vaguely gratuitous could slip insidiously into the category of the eminently desirable. Prudent budgeting was the only way. Putting two university salaries together did not warrant unlimited spending.

At that moment she'd thought, putting two salaries together, that's his image of marriage. Those two plainly delineated entities joining, separating, copulating, uniting against unforeseen encroachments—like a diagram in a textbook. At which thought a small hint of mutiny stirred in her mind.

But surely no mutiny on that last night because after they'd given the waitress their order she said why didn't they go the next afternoon to look for what they'd decided must be a new dining table. A mahogany one to go with George's mahogany sideboard. George waited till he finished his cocktail. "Celia, I'm going on a trip."

"Yes, darling. A week from Thursday."

But it turned out he didn't mean the honeymoon, which was to be two weeks in Spain, and for which a travel agent had already made the (prudently budgeted) arrangements. He was going to see the family of his old friend Roy Ellsworth.

"Roy. Isn't he the one who died two years ago?"

That was it.

"Sort of late for a condolence call."

"This is a birthday party." George started on his lamb stew as he explained. Roy's father was Professor Eric Ellsworth—English department and before her time, though since he was so distinguished perhaps she'd heard the name. At any rate, George had just remembered that his birthday, which was always an auspicious family occasion, was on July tenth. More auspicious this year because by his rough computations, this birthday was the professor's eightieth. The family was sure to be there.

"Where is there?"

"Cedar Springs, Vermont. Where Roy and I went to prep school. Also, where Ellsworth has lived since his retirement."

She did a quick calculation: George's prep school—is he really talking about a period forty years back? "Who's the family?"

"Roy left a wife, Madeleine, I believe her name is, and four children. Ages roughly thirty-one to seventeen."

She glanced over at the next table. The hot Boston summer had set in; the two women on their left were wearing shorts and sleeveless blouses. "George, I'll come. Must be a beautiful drive—I can get the day off."

Another pause while he buttered a roll. Then he said he

3

didn't plan to go for just a day. It might take two days or even three.

Something about his voice made her look at him. The square head was bent downward, the pale eyes stared at the table, the mouth gave an unaccustomed twitch. *What* might take three days?—his pose deterred the question. Instead she said, "George, a high-school friend, someone you haven't seen all these years, you can't have been close to if you don't even know his wife. . . ."

He waved his fork. "That's not the point. We felt close. Once every couple of years I called him, sometimes he called me. I don't have to know the family, I know *about* them; in friendship that's what counts."

"But still. Forty years . . ."

"Roy and I were best friends all through high school. Actually, I was his only friend. The only one, over that long period, he ever really talked to." Still that portentous voice.

Well, lots of men have some experience that casts a glow over the whole rest of their lives: the time they shook hands with the vice president, or trained for the Olympics, or were on a plane that made an emergency landing. With George it was high school. He had made his mark as a professor of mathematics, many years ago he had been married and divorced, he traveled around the world to give well-received papers at academic conferences, but sometimes she thought nothing could match the place in his heart reserved for his four years at Cedar Springs Preparatory School. Once he described for her the physical set-up of the place. "Put a blindfold on me today and I still could find my way around. Forty steps to Russell Hall. Eighty-five and two left turns to the gym. Thirty-three to the dorm where Roy and I lived our last two years."

She asked him to tell her about Roy.

George wiped his lips. "Ellsworth divorced his mother when Roy was two or three. The legend was she'd been running around—well, she couldn't have been an angel be-

4

cause Ellsworth got custody. Anyhow, couple of years after that, he married someone else. A woman with money. Real money. She was heiress to some food-processing fortune, I think. She died in a car accident when Roy was ten."

"Not such a stable childhood for your high-school buddy."

Agreed.

"Well, anyhow, they must all be rich."

George shook his head. "Wasn't like that. Not for Roy or, for that matter, his father. At least he never lived like a rich man. He kept teaching here till retirement age, now he's sick and lives in their old vacation house—well, one of their half-dozen vacation houses, it must have been—in Cedar Springs."

"So the money is still there, getting bigger, the way money does when you leave it alone."

"I suppose it is." George folded his lips: discussion ended.

She bent over her plate. Odd. George was not normally secretive, just the opposite; he held candor to be a moral obligation. Easy for him to follow his own precepts: he prided himself on being a man with nothing to hide. If you have an idea, come out with it, he would say. Or, lay all the facts on the table, that's the only way you'll get a handle on them. Sometimes, as he divested himself of one outspoken notion after another, she pictured him as cleaning out the corners of his mind the way a housewife obsessively cleans out corners of the attic.

Only here he is with a trip that has not just an obscure rationale but an indeterminate schedule. Could take two or three days—George, whose clothes are always laid out the night before, who knows in June what he will ask on the final exam next January, who'd been horrified at her idea of travel, which was just sort of to make up your mind as you went along.

Then she thought of something. "Day after tomorrow,

isn't that when we're supposed to put down the deposit on the apartment? So if you're not here I'll go alone."

He neatly apportioned meat and potatoes on his fork. Then he said maybe they should wait.

"But George, you know what they said, no later than Wednesday morning."

Another meticulous spoonful. "The house is still available. I called this afternoon."

She didn't have to ask which house he meant. The place that aroused that look of exalted desire on his face, perhaps the only thing in the world to do so. After their last visit, George had sat down with paper and pencil and made two lists. On one side their two salaries—those textbook diagrams—preparing for union; on the other, a list of expenses—all the validation of his theorem that two could not live as cheaply as one. When the two sides failed to coincide, that was the end. He never mentioned the house again. They began taking measurements of the pleasant apartment.

Only here he is: the house. "George, how come?"

"Maybe we'll be able to swing it."

"George, did something happen, are they giving you a raise, did a great aunt die, will you rob a bank?"

She spoke in a jocular tone, unprepared for the sober look on his face. Just wait, was what he said. See what develops.

"Develops how? George, what is all this?"

"All I mean is, they won't rent that apartment so fast, hold off with the deposit till I come back." He put his hand over hers. "Celia, you liked the house too, didn't you?"

Well, that distinctive place, Gothic Revival style, with its ornamented verandas, pointed dormers, steep central gable—how could one not like it? It slid into her mind, all the picturesque and endearing details, as she'd seen it from the car window when they drove away for the last time—what, then, was giving her that acute twinge of displeasure? Then she understood. There was an extra detail she hadn't noticed: figures on the porch. George and Celia. The two of them together, year in, year out. An impermeable duo.

George was talking. "Tell you what you could do while I'm gone. That hotel we picked for Seville—I was reading one of the guide books, there seem to be two others equally good and a lot cheaper; could be we let the travel agent con us into something. So if you could do a little research . . ."

She put down her fork. "George, I can't marry you."

"Celia, no jokes, please."

"I'm sorry. I really can't. I . . . well, I can't."

"Celia, dear, talk sense." His calmly professorial tone. The one invaluable for at once disabusing a student of a wrong answer and leading him down the path to the right one.

"Oh, please don't make it harder."

"Is it something with the house? You don't want to commute? Too far out in the country? Too much responsibility? Forget it, we'll take the apartment."

"Nothing to do with where we live. It's just—well, I just realized." She saw him look over at the next table, where the two women in their sleeveless blouses were silent, half turned in their direction. Did she talk too loud? Was there a special look emanating from their faces to signify to strangers that a crisis was in progress? But as though he had not yet fully appropriated the information, George's face was set in purposeful dignity as he said it was a funny time for that kind of realization.

"The department is giving us a tea this Sunday. We have the University Chapel reserved for three to four on Thursday. Travel Limited has us booked in five different—"

"George, I couldn't be more sorry."

True enough. Not sorry to have said it, but devastated by the idea of putting him through so squalid an ordeal. Couldn't she have paid tribute to his stature with some more eloquent approach? After all, a distinguished professor of higher mathematics, to have to hear this in a restaurant with the lamb stew congealing in grease in front of him, and people at the next table looking over, and the inescapable thought that anywhere around might be colleagues and students. Hey, isn't that Theroux, and that must be the dame he's going to marry—intolerable. If only there were some way to make it easy for him, confer on them both a kindly invisibility. Maybe if she stood up now, pretended she didn't feel well. No, he would ascribe her words to a temporary aberration.

In fact, he was doing it now. Girls got skittish at the approach of marriage, he said with an air of great indulgence. Standard syndrome. He could understand.

"George, I'm thirty-five. I've been married before. I'm no blushing bride. I know my own mind."

"Pity you didn't know it a month ago." Still equable, however.

Well, he had her there. Fair enough. She was the one now to reach out a hand, which he shook off as soon as it touched him. "I feel terrible. If only I could just undo the last four weeks."

"You know what you won't be able to undo? The mistake you're making now," and his tone all at once was not equable or even professorial at all, it sounded a new ugly note. "You think you'll like being alone? Think again, my dear woman. Because where are you going to find someone else? It's not as if you were on the teaching staff. Or even one of those doctoral candidates, the halls are full of them, snappy girls who wrangle their fellowships year after year and nothing to do but make eyes at the professors. That's what you're up against," he said in his new voice of complacent spite. "Your competition. You're not even so young. Oh, good looks now, I admit, that nice brown hair and the size eight figure—most commendable, but how long do you think they'll last? Thirty-five, did you say? Come now, Celia. Closer to thirty-six, I have it written down. . . . Okay, okay, twenty years younger than I am, but for a woman in the marriage market, that's close to being leftover goods. Odd lot. Ready to be marked down. You'll start to understand what it means."

He stopped, but only to wipe the corners of his mouth. "Or maybe you figure you can opt out of that uncongenial market. You can support yourself, after all. That little section of the administration office you run—what do they call it again?"

Don't talk. He knows perfectly well what they call it.

"Special Projects. Yes. Making sure there are enough cookies at the tea for incoming freshmen. Seeing that graduation doesn't come on the same day as the football awards dinner. Oh, it's necessary, I grant you, someone has to do it, but does it really have anything to do with what makes a university great?"

She folded her hands on the table. Imagine, she might have married him, a man capable of such vindictiveness, of churning out these venomous statements with that look of pedantic calm.

On the other hand, maybe if she'd married him this trait would never have surfaced, they could have jogged on together year after year without her knowing about it. Like heroism, maybe. If I just had something to challenge me, the world would see how courageous and noble and daring I could be—don't people think this all the time while following with hesitant footsteps life's undemanding course? Well, maybe George's malevolence was like that. Had he not sat here in a restaurant and heard something to wound him, shatter his pride, the trait would have stayed forever hidden—lost, unreal, unexercised.

He sat in meditative silence. Anyone looking? Note the serene gaze, the steady mouth: portrait of a satisfied diner giving himself to the pleasure of appreciative digestion. But when his eyes met hers, she detected in them an unaccustomed gleam. "I know. It's Jason, isn't it? Jason Bailey. I didn't pay attention when they told me, but now I understand."

They: anyone connected with the university. Like a big family, you sometimes heard, with the tacit addendum that family sanctioned unremitting watchfulness, inescapable contiguity.

"Well, Celia, get wise to yourself. Jason Bailey, the English department's hotshot bachelor—you don't stand a chance on that front. Walk by his office sometime if you don't believe. A dozen of them always standing there. Graduate groupies. All of them desperate for that fifteen minutes alone with Professor Bailey."

She tried not to show her shock. Even his language: Get wise to yourself—That fastidious George, who weighs every mannered word . . . from what hitherto undisclosed depths is he pulling these? "Listen. I don't know who told you what, but I was with Jason Bailey exactly twice. He came to the office—that office you say does such trivial stuff—anyhow, he wanted to check on the date for some conference his department is running next fall. And while we were going over the calendar, he said suppose we do this over coffee . . ." She stopped. It's too degrading. Besides, Jason does figure in. No, not Jason exactly. Anyone who was open, easy, to point up for whatever part of her mind was receptive to contrast with George's tightness. Or maybe it was Jason himself, Jason who gave his irreverent view of that fall conference, any conference, as they walked down the steps of Atwater Hall, Jason who marveled that every event of importance to the university for the next five years could be tucked into one pretty head, Jason who said since neither of us has to be someplace fast, can't we string this out another hour. Maybe it was, maybe it was.

"And don't think you can change your mind." Still at it. "A little backtracking with George for auld lang syne. You had a good run for the money, but this is it. The finish line. Celia, you look puzzled—let me elucidate. If you're sitting home alone some night, and the phone doesn't ring, and you spot a gray hair in with those luscious brown ones, don't think you can just do an about face. Whatever it is you have in mind. Little Sunday night supper. Two tickets for an open air concert. Walk along the river—isn't that how we started? Well, save your breath. George won't be there, that line is cut."

It's her fault. In some private place, her apartment, his apartment, his fury could materialize into something physical, some alleviating violence: a dish smashed, a chair hurled, even the traditional slaps across a face. Instead, poor wretched man, he has to sit with his look of preternatural calm: the professor conscious of his public as he gives his exegesis on the nature of ill will.

At least they don't have to drag it out any longer; no way for this session to go except down, she thought, as with a sprightly wave for that putative public, a jaunty pretense that everything was all right, she stood and walked out of the restaurant. But despite what he said about the line being cut—another unlikely phrase from his stately stock—for all that explosion of disgust and spite, he won't want this ugly scene to be the last word. He's a civilized man, after all; decent, honorable; all his instincts are kindly, caring. And the two of them did, as he said, have something good going for a while. Tonight, alone with his books, his framed diplomas, his staid furniture, he'll swing around to some face-saving rationalization. It would never have worked out. She was not my type. A woman without an academic background. Pride will be restored by tomorrow, at which time he'll call or she'll call; with both of them putting in their best effort, they'll patch up something for those avid watchers, some formula that abjures blame and confers dignity. Both decided . . . mutual . . . great respect . . . happy. After this shabby exhibition, an ending that's awkward but decent: leave it to George to arrange it.

But by tomorrow, of course, George was dead.

2

"MAYBE SOME OF IT you're just imagining," Jason said.

She looked across the table at him. They were in a coffee shop two blocks from campus because her office had provided no privacy. Though she took the unprecedented step, when she came in this morning, of closing her door between nine and nine-thirty, fifteen people had provided themselves with a pretext to open it. Jason was the sixteenth, but him, she found she wanted to talk to.

"No imagining. I'm one of the sights. Obligatory stop on the University Tour. Woman who can be held responsible for George Theroux's death." She put down her cup. "Oh, Jason, obviously it's not like that. Did anyone actually say, Celia, old girl, by your callousness and tactlessness you killed him? Not quite. But the dean said, If only we could know in advance what the results of our actions would be. Two professors in his department looked me coldly in the eye and said it was a great blow to scholarship. His teaching assistant said he knew how much George had been looking forward to being married. A friend of mine, someone I thought was a friend, said, Celia, you poor dear, of course if you'd known, you'd never have done it."

"All that by nine-thirty this morning?" Jason shook his head.

"Look. If a prominent professor says the wedding is off,

12

and then tells his staff he's going on a trip, and then shoots himself when he gets there—I mean, that's the kind of news to get around fast."

"How come everyone knew the engagement was broken?"

"Because first thing yesterday morning before he left he made eight phone calls. Eight that I know of. To the minister who was going to marry us, to the grounds superintendent who'd engaged the chapel, to his best friend who was giving us a cocktail party after the wedding, to the second best friend who was taking us out to dinner after that, to his brother who lives in Chicago and arranged his vacation around the wedding, to the travel agent . . . how many am I up to?"

"Far as they were concerned, could have been a mutual decision."

"Uh, uh. Celia ditched me: evidently he came right out with it. All the facts on the table—George all over."

Jason murmured something—he was sorry?—but what she heard, what still rang in her ear, was the voice on the phone last night bringing her the news. Someone from the math department, who had heard from the president's office, who got a call from the police chief of Cedar Springs, Vermont: George Theroux found behind the Cedar Springs Inn with a lethal bullet wound in his chest and a gun in his hand. Everything simple at that point. Standing alone in her living room, a great lament in her heart for the man she'd made love to countless times right in that apartment, the man whose interests and problems and habits she'd contemplated taking on for life. But by today, having been exposed to the remonstrative public, having felt the force of their censorious and prurient sympathy, she was buffeted by feelings that were disparate, even contradictory. Relief, vast relief, at no longer being committed to marriage with George, anguish at the idea that at fifty-five he was dead, resentment of those who held her accountable for this death, understanding of why in their minds she should be held to this accountability—the emotions swayed within her, unbalancing her, so when she looked up at the restaurant ceiling it seemed to her that the light fixture in its garish pink case was shaking. And added to this inner confusion was the thought that she shouldn't be sitting here with Jason, that under the circumstances it had been impolitic to walk with him down the hall and across the campus, at the same time as she realized that she liked sitting here with him; she was getting the first comfort of the day.

"And another thing," she said. "I work in administration. It's a hard job, I earn my keep, but you academics are snobs—don't make a face, it's true." Making sure there are enough cookies at the tea for incoming freshmen. "Anyone who doesn't teach is a cut below the cloth. I should've been grateful to have a professor, a real professor, give me the nod."

"Celia, that's—"

"You know what? If I were an academic they'd forgive me. I'd be a serious person. I'd be entitled to have made a small mistake. Or even if . . ." Her hand twirled the coffee cup round and round. "If I weren't so . . . I mean, if I were a frump. Someone with stringy hair and a scrawny face. Anything except that glamour puss in administration who seduced a nice professor and then meanly let him down."

Jason's gaze went over her. Then all he said, with an air of distinctness, was that she sure as hell could not be described as a frump.

"I don't know. They make me feel so . . . indelicate."

"In my book, there's never been any indelicacy about a woman's being good-looking." Another glance across the table. "Anyhow, stop brooding about your misfortune in having a classy face and tell me about George. Had he at any time been depressed?"

"George! Depressed!" She finished the muffin she had not expected to eat at all. "He was too sure of himself. His aim in life was to be a first-rate math professor, and he was a first-rate math professor. The kind of self-doubt that brings on depression just wasn't part of his makeup."

"How about feeling—I hate to use the word 'alienated' but I will use it."

"Not that either. Why should he be? He had plenty of colleagues who respected him and liked him and agreed with him that things were just about the way they should be."

"How about when you told him? What was his reaction then?"

He put that clever mind of his to devising the cruelest of taunts. Leftover goods. Not one of those snappy doctoral candidates. Gray hair in that luscious brown. That little section of administration. . . . She can't say any of it. There's no neat paraphrase with which to convey malice while still leaving inviolate the one maligned.

"He was very angry," she said, and gasped at her own oversimplification. "He said—he was right, of course—I should have known earlier. Before we'd signed up for the chapel and gone looking at places to live and spent all those evenings with the guide books." Outside in the street, a truck was pulling in backwards and she fixed her gaze on it. "Now you mention it, his upset wasn't so much at losing me as at lousing up arrangements. He liked his schedules to be set. Everything orderly and down pat. Only there I was, turning all the carefully laid plans upside down."

Jason nodded. "That squares with the image I have. Someone didactic, settled, conservative, no great excess of sensibility—Celia, forgive me. I didn't mean to knock him."

"Jason, you forget. This is the man I decided *not* to marry."

"Anything else about his reaction?"

"Well, he was always very stiff about language. Every sentence suitable for presentation in front of a classroom.

But sitting there at the restaurant . . ." This is better. If she dwells on the style of that ugly harangue, perhaps she can ignore the substance. "I don't know. A different George. He sounded—see that fellow standing against the car? No, that way, in front of the grocer's. So if he had a blowup with his girl—I mean, a snarling outburst like that."

Jason sat silent. Did he suspect that he played a role in that outburst? Could that possibly figure into his speculation? When he spoke, his tone was decisive. "In short, the reaction of an exasperated man, but not of the deeply unhappy one who plans to do away with himself, would you say?"

She drew a deep breath. It was of course what she'd been wanting someone else to say: that George was not by any stretch of the imagination a candidate for suicide. But you couldn't exactly ask someone to say it. You surely couldn't when the world was engaged in a judgmental exercise against you, and the effort to reinterpret a man's death could be taken as the desire to disparage his memory. Only now, over empty coffee cups on a fake marble table, Jason has said it. Or at least, moving inch by persuasive inch, he has got them to the point where it no longer has to be said.

Then from Jason another question. How did the suicide rumor get started?

"Easy. When the police called the university and asked for information, whoever answered told them Mr. Theroux's engagement had been broken the day before. So this added to the fact that the only thing he was known to have done in Cedar Springs was the morbid act of taking a solitary walk around his old prep school . . ."

"Right. And the Cedar Springs police force, like a police force anywhere, was glad to seize on a supposition that seemed to let them off a difficult hook."

"Then what you're saying . . . I mean, if he didn't kill himself."

She saw her hand shake on the cup. Suicide at least has

the connotation of reasonableness. It comes trailing a long tradition. It plays a part in the annals of any university. However destructive it is to those left behind, you understand how intelligent men—not a particular man, maybe, but men in general—can opt for it. But if that hypothesis is brushed aside, there's no way you can prepare yourself for the vista that opens in its place.

Who in the world would want to kill George? She thought it and then forced herself to say it. "That orderly life—it wasn't scheduled for enemies. His divorce was amicable and anyhow it happened twenty years ago, and he wasn't working on some great mathematical theory to knock them cold and make a colleague jealous, and he hadn't just given a football star a failing grade, and if he was feuding with someone, it was a secret from me this past year."

"Celia, you need more coffee." Jason beckoned to the waitress. Without having to discuss it, they had chosen this place for its drabness—trust the university crowd to pass it by. He waited till her cup was filled, then he asked about the trip to Cedar Springs.

"I don't know. George didn't explain. He just said he was going to see Roy Ellsworth's family."

"Roy. Would that be Professor Ellsworth's son?"

"Um, hmm."

"Ellsworth. He was the main reason I decided to come here when I started working for my degree fifteen years ago."

Well, of course. Jason had a life too: he wrote papers, applied for fellowships, sweated out the tenure process—she realized it with a shock. That's what happens when you're involved in a disaster: everyone experienced simply as an adjunct, a prop, someone with benign feelings and infinite attention on whom theories about your predicament can be tested. Egocentricity claims you, as it does an invalid. You have only one basis for judgment: will his participation help me or hurt me? But in fact there was a real person sitting opposite her: open face, concerned gaze, the kind of large loose-jointed frame that makes a point just standing in front of a classroom. The English department's hotshot bachelor—George meant to be vituperative, but really, what's so bad about it?

"Great teacher, Ellsworth," Jason said. "The best. Actually, once I wanted to slug him. I remember his exact words. Jason, just because you're our favorite graduate student does not mean you can hand in a paper with a confused theme and rambling exposition and two dangling participles besides. Took me a month to stop feeling peevish and have the sense to be grateful." He looked up. "So now tell me why George went visiting there."

"It was Ellsworth's birthday and he figured the family would be around."

"But didn't I hear that Roy Ellsworth died of cancer two years ago?"

"Right. And George didn't even know the family. He went to prep school with Roy, they were buddies, and after that they sort of kept in desultory touch, the way high-school buddies do. What I'm saying, he didn't know them, but he wanted to see them. Why? All of a sudden, a week before his wedding, why does he want a visit with the Ellsworths?"

She looked out through the dirt-smudged windows: starting to rain. "And then the timing. Two or three days. George, that rigid scheduler. I once said to him, did we have to decide now, in Boston, how long we'd stay in Barcelona, and he looked at me as if I was some dissolute woman. To not have the strength of character to decide four weeks in advance at what hour you would want to leave a city. Jason, don't ask me any more, I just don't know." The waitress was hovering—more coffee?—but Celia shook her head. "Actually, I do know something. I just realized. I wasn't paying attention, I was preoccupied with how I was going to tell him about—you know. But now I think back, something odd."

Jason waited.

"George was longing to buy a place in the country. Twenty-three acres and orchards and an authentic barn with every beam intact and a pond—all that plus some very good Gothic Revival architecture. I don't know—it appealed to some romantic strain you wouldn't have thought he had. The math professor as gentleman farmer. Except he couldn't afford it. He did hours of careful computation, his salary, my salary, upkeep, taxes, caretaker, the lot, and he said he couldn't afford it. But there we were at dinner and possibly he could afford it."

"But what's that got to do with the trip?"

"The two things were juxtaposed, you see, in his mind. First the announcement about two or three days in Vermont—that was shocker enough—and then the second shocker that maybe after all he could swing the house. And as I said, I was in my own world, a compelling one, how do you say something ugly and make it come out sweet. . . ." She watched the waitress put down orders on the next table. "Now I see. It was something up there. Obviously. A week before his wedding, George wasn't fixing to go see the beauties of Vermont. He had a scheme in mind, some plan to get him money. But the family didn't like it, so they took him walking behind the inn—"

"Hey, Celia, go easy. You can't exactly convict people long distance."

That worried look on his face—she's gone too fast. She sighed and asked him to tell her about Professor Ellsworth.

"A private man and a very proud one. I cared about him a lot." A new look for Jason—tender, earnest. "Also, I didn't exactly understand him, none of us did. He'd inherited a fortune from his wife—George told you?—and there he was teaching till retirement age. Past it. A man with that kind of bankroll, going over term papers and lecturing twice a week on the Romantic poets and turning out scholarly footnotes for meetings of the M.L.A.—the stuff university myths are made of."

"When did he retire?"

"Eight or nine years ago; this must be his eightieth birthday coming up. Not a very healthy eighty. Proud, did I say? Pride holds him together. But he's had two heart attacks and also there was some vascular problem a couple of years ago, they had to amputate a leg. Actually . . ."

She waited. On that expressive face, another shift.

"I have a letter from him in my pocket. Came yesterday."

"Jason, a letter about what? Why didn't you tell me?"

"He asks me to send him someone—here, you read it."

She opened the envelope. "'Have to forgive an old man's typing. I can no longer see well enough to read back what my fingers have set down. . . .' Good God. Blind also."

Jason nodded. "Someone like him, unable to read—I've been trying to cross it out."

"So he wants someone—let's see. 'Person will have to transcribe my words on a tape recorder and type them up, meanwhile perhaps smoothing out the rough edges inevitable with dictation, and then read them back to me so I am in a position to make further corrections . . .' I think I know why you didn't tell me."

"Celia, I was considering it."

She looked over the rest. "'Since I'm not up to interviewing people myself, Jason, I'll trust your judgment. Just send someone agreeable and talented who wants to make some extra money during a month of summer—a person with the patience to put up with an old man's crotchets and the intelligence to savor his ideas.'" She stared out the window: the fellow typecast to break up with his girl still leaning against the car. "I have to go up there," she said slowly. "It's the only thing that makes sense. I can turn it over and over here and I'll never get anyplace. But if I'm on the spot, if I can talk to those people and see the place where it happened and go to that school he walked around in. But I can't look as if I'm doing that. So if I had a bona fide job, if everyone knew I was there for a job. I mean, there's no way I can just be snooping around. Celia Sommerville, girl detective—not exactly my style."

Her offhand voice, but in fact she saw herself playing exactly that daring and flashy role. Clues, sly prodding, insights, guesses—the whole paraphernalia of canny discovery in order to nail down that family Jason had said she must not condemn in advance. And after that, from everyone here at home, the satisfying denouement. Celia, forgive us. Celia, we misjudged you. Oh, Miss Sommerville, we should have known there was something funny about that trip.

Still skeptical, Jason was watching her. What about a funeral? Won't she want to be here for that?

"There'll be a memorial service in the fall—the dean has it set up already. As for the burial or cremation or whatever one does, his brother is there now, he'll attend to that."

"Can't you trust his brother to ask the proper questions?" Jason, still pushing prudence, circumspection.

"Not likely. I could tell from talking to him on the phone he doesn't think there are questions to be asked. George committed suicide because callous Celia broke his heart—that's it."

Will this satisfy Jason's objections? Not quite. How can she leave her job for a month, he asked.

"I was taking off four weeks anyhow. Two for the, um, honeymoon, two after that to get us settled." When she put down her cup, coffee spilled on the table. "Besides, I want to get away from here, I have to. If they feel critical toward me, I'm even more angry at them. All of them. All these good bright learned people who jumped to the facile conclusion without knowing a damn thing. They don't want to know, why clutter up those intelligent minds. And I don't intend to tell them. I mean, if you think I'm going to spend the summer making the case that George really didn't, he couldn't have, that never in a million years. Honestly, I'd be the one to kill myself before I'd try selling that defense. No, Jason, it's all right, I'm not hysterical." But she's yelling, she must be, why else would people at the counter be swiveling on their stools to look at her?

She waited till her breath was steady, then she said there was something else. "One of the deans mentioned firing me. Okay, he didn't say it like that. Bad mark in the public eye, was what he said. Usefulness possibly at an end. What he meant was, if it gets to be accepted that I'm the cause of George's death, I'm out on my ear. How do you like that! Six years in that office, and I'm out. Oh, he'd have a fight on his hands, the union would back me, but then again maybe they wouldn't, they'd think if you make a man kill himself you shouldn't be the one lining up speakers for baccalaureate day. And it's not like I'm a professor who has tenure; you have to rape three girls in a broom closet before there are grounds for firing."

"Celia, take it easy."

"Right." She started reading the rest of the letter. "'Since ill health has cut down on my mobility and advanced age has discouraged housekeeping, I'll provide living quarters for whomever you send at a pretty country inn some ten blocks from where I live. He or she will have a corner room, every comfort, and if I remember correctly from when I ventured out some years back, excellent New England cooking.' Sounds like the hotel where George was."

"Only one in town, probably."

"'Perchance'—perchance, I love him already—'perchance your candidate will find some interest in the subject I propose to discuss. Fringe benefit.'" She sighed. "I've always said it was a disgrace how little literature I know, so maybe this is my chance to catch up."

"His last book was on *King Lear*. No, *Coriolanus*. No,

Lear is right. Celia, you may be getting into more than you bargain for."

"You mean I won't be able to follow a retired professor's discussion of *King Lear*?"

But in the concentrated silence of their suddenly exchanged glances, it was clear they both understood this was not what he meant.

3

WELL, IT WASN'T ABOUT *King Lear* that Professor Ellsworth intended to talk. Nothing like it—he made that clear right away. "I trust you're interested in children," was what he said after they'd got through the business of introductions. "Oh, Miss Sommerville, don't be worried. Not real children. I didn't get you here under false pretenses, to wipe noses and button sweaters of obstreperous five-year-olds. But in a sense these are real children too. Children in books—real, at least, to me."

When he stopped to take a breath she had a chance to observe him. The lines crisscrossing his face, the veins blue and bloated on his hands, the head wobbly on a rubbery neck—he looked older than eighty. He was sitting in a large leather chair, and though the warmest of July breezes came through the windows, he kept a blanket over his legs. Or—she remembered what Jason had told her—what remained of his legs. It was the image she had of her grandfather: tired and crafty and also mildly truculent, as if on guard against all the influences inimical to his well-being.

"So. Our summer project. Children. What makes them act the way they do? How much can you blame on parents? How much can parents blame on the mandates of their time? How much would have happened anyhow? I was reading two articles the other day. Distinguished thinkers, both of them. One said the punitive upbringing given our forefathers in this country made them sufficiently brash and resolute so they would not put up with the authority of an overseas king. The other said the punitive upbringing given a generation in Germany made them sufficiently cowed and submissive so they welcomed the authority of Hitler. Fascinating, isn't it? Same equation, different answers. Anyone with a family may well brood on it. Mine happens to be a fine family, splendid people, but it doesn't always turn out like that. Why not? What makes the difference? Well, when a professor of literature feels the need of insight, what does he turn to? Literature, of course. You don't think that's so strange? You're a bright young woman, you must be, otherwise Professor Bailey would not have sent you. Good-looking too. Oh, I can tell. My eyesight is no longer sufficient to let me read, but it still sends me signals about an attractive woman. I didn't specify it, Miss Sommerville, but I'm glad Jason had the sense.

"Incidentally, must I call you Miss Sommerville? Celia, then, such a pretty name." The veined hands clasped and unclasped. "They made you comfortable at that inn, I trust? Gave you a nice room? Pleasant people, the managers, I hope they treat my other guests as well. You look startled. My family is here to spend a few days and celebrate my birthday. The truth is, I asked them to come—an old man's command performance. One of the perks of advancing age: you can indulge in that kind of imperious request once in a while."

Startled—is that how she looked? She'd better watch it: she meant simply to show interest. And actually, if she was here to look out for the family, they were on the lookout for her. Or at least for someone in her position—Mrs. Roy Ellsworth had come over to her last night when she was standing in the lobby.

She was a large woman with even features and a great mass of reddish brown hair, and she spoke with vehement friendliness. She had heard that her father-in-law had hired a young woman from that same University as a certain Mr. Theroux who . . . Ah, yes. So Celia knew about that sad event. What she deduced when she saw the name and address in the register. Well, what she wanted to tell the newcomer was that they weren't letting the professor know about George Theroux's death. Mr. Theroux had been an old school friend of her husband's. Her late husband, Roy, who died two years ago. "The police have agreed," she added. "A man, after all, who's had two heart attacks, it's incumbent on all of us to be careful."

Celia leaned against the counter, where the register now was closed. "Won't he read it in the local paper?"

"If you're working for him, you must know he can't read a newspaper."

In the wrong before she has even started. Celia murmured that she forgot.

"And then no phone in his room—long ago he stipulated that—not even a TV, so no danger there. And the young man who takes care of him—his name is Lester—he understands the importance. So there should be no problem." Then Mrs. Ellsworth's gaze sharpened; were there other problems? "Such a wretched business, that poor George Theroux. You can't help wondering how a thing like that could happen."

True enough: you really can't.

"For a man in his prime, one who has everything to live for, to just go out and shoot himself."

So it is a confrontation. During her first half hour, a confrontation with the very theory she is here to discredit.

Mrs. Ellsworth had busy eyes that seemed able to take in the activity in the lobby and also to keep Celia in precise focus. "I know a little about suicide. My husband Roy was sick for several years. Cancer of the esophagus. The worst. Well, I suppose any form of that terrible disease is the worst. So if those who suffer turn their minds to some way of ending it, you can't blame them. I won't pretend that Roy was exempt. Of course the temptation was there. To take too much of the medicines, or skip the medicines altogether, or prevail on a compliant doctor. But he resisted it. I admired that. He really did resist it. While he was thinking about opting out, he was also plotting how he could manage to live for another twelve months, six months, one month. We even went down to Mexico. One of those wonder treatments that turns out to be not such a wonder, but the point is, he tried. He was in there fighting. The tests, the consultations, the old medicines, the new medicines. He even made himself an authority. My husband, the manufacturer of ladies' handbags, an expert on the treatment of cancer of the esophagus."

The alert eyes looked sideways, where the last of the diners were coming out of the dining room. "So then you have a man who went to school with him, an old friend, and he does just the opposite. Holds life so cheap he kills himself. But first he does something so odd as to visit their old school—Look. You're busy. I'm keeping you from something."

Celia said she was not too busy.

"I have a theory about that school visit—sure you want to hear this?"

I'm sure I ought to hear it. Another nod.

"My theory is he was in some kind of crisis. Something cataclysmic to disorganize him. Typical of those contemplating suicide. But unconsciously he was also looking for someone to stop him. An intervening agent. That's why he was at the school. Waiting for someone to grab him by the back of the neck and say, What is all this, or Come, come now, let's talk about it. The way they intervened in the old student days. But of course no one did. Even though he stood around—this was in the papers—for half an hour, no one said, Come, come now. So the poor man returned here. Maybe I shouldn't be talking to you so freely. Just because you have that interested look."

The wild thought crossed her mind that she was being hypnotized. Can you be hypnotized in a hotel lobby, where a few feet away a couple stand reading a bird book, and a father tells his son they're going up now, and at the desk a man says look again, he knows the letter must have come? And can it be performed, moreover, by an operator whose tone is didactic rather than murmurous, and whose concentration on your face is absolute even while she manages to concentrate on everything else going on around?

"Then the place, the very beautiful place, where he did it. Down by the brook. Have you seen it? Oh, you must go, one of the heavenly spots. That seems odd to people too. Why didn't he do it in his own home, everyone says. My own children say it. But I think I understand. In his own home there would have been restraints. His papers. His furniture. His pictures. His clothes. You know what the books call all that? The psychic force of normalcy—those experts, amazing what words they come up with. But no restraints down there by the brook, nothing to stop him from pulling out a gun and shooting himself."

Yes, definitely a form of hypnosis. To keep from sliding under, she looked down at the counter, where brochures listing the treats available to guests at the Cedar Springs Inn were displayed. At a distance of just a few miles, they could visit a workroom where pottery was designed and glazed and fired, they could attend a demonstration, complete with audiovisual effects, of the steps involved in making maple syrup, they could choose one of the three trails—beginner, moderate, difficult—up the nearest mountain. Or they could simply sit on the porch and let their gaze wander past the pink geraniums in their white painted boxes, out, out, over rooftops, church steeples, chimneys, to where that climbable mountain and half a dozen others stood immutable against the sky.

"You won't forget, will you, about not telling the professor? About that wretched death, I mean. Heaven forbid a man in his condition should have a shock."

But now, looking at the figure under the plaid blanket, she thought it wouldn't be such a shock. He could take it. Old people don't mind the deaths of others, especially when the cause is some mishap that has no connection with them. Just by virtue of having lived so long, they've developed a detachment: what doesn't revolve around them doesn't count. It's their own mortality that troubles them, the sense of the threats against their own fragile being.

"You're ready then?" he said. "That neat box, that your tape recorder? So Celia, what books do we start with? Which of the great early novelists write about children?"

She sat stiffly on her upright chair. Her first day, and he'll decide she's unequipped; he should not have relied on Jason for his choice.

"You can't think of any? With good reason. There are none. Tom Jones is an infant wrapped in coarse linen, and then he is a gallant youth ready for lovemaking. Clarissa is a young lady when she decides to defy Papa. Pamela, though but fifteen and called 'child' by her master, by virtue of her working-class origins qualifies as full grown. And a Jane Austen heroine is surely past the age of childhood when she starts on the hunt for a husband that constitutes the serious business of life.

"Why is that, you may ask. Why no view of the child in early fiction? Simple. The concepts in which to talk about childhood don't exist because right through the eighteenth century a child is merely a creature who is not yet an adult; it isn't expected that he develop as a child; rather, it's perceived that he does ineptly what as a grown-up he'll do much better. In short, a miniature adult: someone undersize, inadequate, troublesome, and just possibly an investment destined to yield future benefits. To put it crassly, the child is someone on the way to becoming something else, which makes of childhood a period en route. Like the scenery viewed from a train window, this period may be picturesque, it may have some points of interest, but it isn't meaningful in itself; what counts is the final destination, which is the grown man."

He tugged at the blanket over his lap. "Something a little too frisky about that last sentence, it's the kind I would cross out were I typing myself. See that you cross it out, Celia."

But though she nodded, she won't cross it out. She likes it. What a wonder he is, the thoughts tumbling out as if they'd been piled up, jumbled together, waiting for a chance to emerge. And such an orderly emergence, no idea jostling any other, each one poised, symmetrical, polished, neat. Not at all what she expected when she saw that frail bluish face—she won't be needed for grammatical emendations here.

"So with all those in the eighteenth century who for good reason neglected to write about children, we're lucky we can turn to one marvelous book that does come clean about the fascinating precinct that is childhood, or at least boyhood. And though it's not a novel—"

"What marvelous book, Grandpa?"

Celia looked up. They must have come quietly up the stairs and along the hall, the large handsome woman and a stout man not quite as tall as she was.

Professor Ellsworth jerked upright. "Marcia, my dear. And Bernard. Come closer, so I can see. I was at their wedding," he told Celia. "Twelve years ago."

"Eleven," Marcia said. She had her mother's large even features and smooth tan skin topped by clouds of well-kept reddish brown hair.

"Marcia, this is Celia Sommerville, who is going to be my professional eyes for the next few weeks. Celia, my granddaughter Marcia and her husband Bernard Lenox." He was still squinting up at them. "So you say eleven years—we won't look back. Except that wedding. What a pleasure to remember that."

"You ought to remember the wedding. The way you danced the tango."

"No!"

"Oh, yes." Marcia's speech was also like her mother's. Vehement, glittering. "With that gorgeous blonde, Bernie's aunt."

"She said you were the best partner she had all evening," Bernard said.

The old man plucked at the blanket. "I won't be dancing the tango any more."

"The loss is to your audience," Bernard nicely said and stood at attention, a pudgy man in a dark blue suit.

"And you made a speech," Marcia added.

"I hope I wasn't indiscreet."

"You were marvelous. You said wonderful things."

"Then I didn't say what I thought. Should I confess? No, Celia, you can stay, it's not private. I thought you were making a great mistake. I told your parents. I said, don't let her do it, she's too young, it will never hold up. All this flitting in and out of marriage, a whole generation with their energy sapped, their years wasted, their life reduced to the trivia of the divorce courts . . . yes, my dear, just what I said. I didn't want that for my granddaughter."

Marcia bent over and kissed him. "You were sweet not to say it."

"The truth is, I didn't trust your car either. That jalopy you drove off in. Green, wasn't it?"

"Handpainted green," Bernard said.

"Some of my hand too," Marcia put in. "I have to admit, Grandpa, you were right about that. The transmission lasted till we got out of the city."

"We found a bus," Bernard said. "From then on we did fine."

They were doing fine now, Celia saw; the clipped routine

went off without a hitch. Professor Ellsworth sat with eyes crinkled, lips smiling: an old man juggling the small bright balls of memory.

From the wedding they moved to the rest of the family. Jerry. Gillian. That cute little Cindy. What a delight to have them here. How he looked forward to more time with them. Making his pitch, the lined face leaned forward, the gnarled hands twisted: this was serious business.

And it didn't need a spectator. This time when she stood, no one pressed her to stay. How about nine-thirty tomorrow morning, was all the professor said as she went to the door. That be too early?

She said nine-thirty was fine and walked slowly back to the hotel, past the stone fences and broad fields and white shingled houses that gave Cedar Springs its picture-postcard quality, and along a brook that wandered first on one side of the road and then, headstrong, sparkling, the other. Mrs. Ellsworth, Marcia, Bernie—not too bad for her first twenty-four hours.

But at dinner her spirits sank. They were at a table not far from her, laughing, exchanging portions—Here, try a bite of this—giving orders to the waitress and in a burst of jollity countermanding them, and she realized her mistake. So easy, she had thought. You asked the sly questions, made the intuitive guesses, ventured down avenues the police were too lazy or too satisfied to negotiate, and you had it.

Well, easy perhaps with one person or even two. But it was five people she was up against, six if you counted Bernie, still out of place, in this bucolic country inn, in a business suit and tie. They were a unit, self-contained, strong, cohesive, trained in exclusivity and mutual support. They even looked alike, Marcia, a younger sister, then the much younger one, all with the same even features and statuesque figures and tawny-colored hair as the mother. It was only the son—Jerry?—whose pallid skin and pinched face set him somewhat apart. Hunched over her solitary leg of lamb, she thought, families, this is what they're for, to resist the intrusion of an outsider.

The outsider stationed herself in the lobby after dinner. In a hotel you have that going for you anyhow: neutral ground where it's permitted to exchange greetings, wrangle connections, work the casual encounter into a full-fledged discussion. The encounter this evening was with Marcia and Bernie.

"There you are, Celia. My grandfather calls you Celia, so I guess we can too."

Sure thing.

"You're really great to do this. Give up a whole month so you can help him."

She said she considered herself lucky to have the job.

When Marcia moved, her white slacks shimmered against long legs. "My mother told me you knew that poor man. Mr. Theroux. The one who—awful, isn't it? A man comes here for a day and shoots himself."

Ah. Another one who is setting her own terms for the discussion. Celia asked if Marcia had met him.

"We all did. He went out of his way to meet us. All those questions."

"What questions?"

"What'd we do and how'd we turn out and he'd heard so much from our father. Even Cindy. You don't know Cindy? That's her, over there. Cindy, come here a sec."

Cindy came reluctantly, with many backward looks at the two teenage boys she'd been talking to. A big girl with her figure encased in a high-school sweatshirt and her face less distinct, when you saw it up close, than her sister's. An adolescent's blur of a face, ready to be defined, in a year or two, by the assurance that marked her sisters and mother.

"Cindy, this is Celia Sommerville. She's working for Grandpa this summer."

"Right on," Cindy said flatly, and turned for another look at her friends.

"You talked to that man, didn't you? Cindy, come on, you know. The one who killed himself."

"Yeah. I guess."

"So what was it like?"

"Like nothing." The unformed face slid into a pout. "He said he went to school with Daddy a million years ago."

"What'd he ask you about? Celia wants to know."

"Freaked me out," Cindy said. "That old guy nosing into my affairs. Like where'd I go to school and how was I doing. As if it's any business of his."

"Cindy, baby, he's *dead*."

"Yeah. Tough." She tugged at the sweatshirt, which was green with white letters. That all Marcia wanted?

"She's a sweet kid," Marcia said as the girl ran back to her friends. "The youngest, we all spoil her, I guess it's only natural. But she really is a sweetheart."

When Celia looked across the lobby, she pictured the encounter: the old guy, his face set in anxious dignity as it stared down into Cindy's impudent, sullen, impatient one. Did he set up an agenda and then, George-fashion, follow it? Was he under the impression that he was ingratiating himself? Did he let his irritation show when Cindy ran off?

And what was it all about anyhow? Celia picked up a magazine—*Trout Fishing*—and asked Marcia if Mr. Theroux had happened to reveal his reason for having come here.

The lobby was getting crowded, as more people came out of the dining room. A father-and-son duo, a woman dressed conspicuously in hiking gear, a couple who'd registered before dinner and now stood at the desk arguing with the clerk. "Mr. Theroux said he wanted to visit his old school," Marcia said. "You heard Cindy. The place he and my father went to ages ago."

"Any reason?"

"No reason," Marcia said.

"Don't need a reason," Bernie dutifully added.

"Sentiment," Marcia said.

"Auld Lang Syne," Bernie added—the vaudeville routine again.

Mrs. Ellsworth was coming out of the dining room. She made her way past the wicker chairs, the tables loaded with magazines, the lamps with clipper ships painted on their shades, but if she saw Celia and her daughter, she gave no sign. "He said he loved the place," Marcia said. "Don't ask me why. I don't think my father liked it all that much. Jesus, high school, I can't even remember my own, who wants to remember. But that Mr. Theroux, he said the best years of his life were there, he remembered every inch. Blindfolded, that's what he said, he could still make his way around."

"Forty steps to Russell Hall. Eighty-five and two left turns to the gym. Thirty-three to the dorm where he and Marcia's father lived." Bernie was reading from a small black notebook he pulled out of a pocket. "I wrote it down. I always try to write down anything interesting. A grown man thinking so much about high school, that has real human interest."

"Well, all that about his past, did it seem to bother him?"

"You mean, was he depressed? Like a man who's going to kill himself? Oh, I get it now." How quickly Marcia could shift, the large features quivering, the reddish brown hair tottering above the distorted face. "You think it's our fault. Something we did. Didn't do. We should have guessed what he had in mind."

"Goodness. Of course not. I just—"

"Sometimes even a psychiatrist can't tell—you hear the horror stories all the time. The doctor says sure, discharge him from the hospital, and that very afternoon, bam. Or it's a phone call, someone wants an appointment, now, please, this minute, and the doctor says can't it wait till Thursday.

Or an office visit, the patient sits there, Fine, fine, no problem, and five minutes after he's left the office, oh, who doesn't know what happens? So how could we be expected, a man we never met before, how did we know if that uptight way of talking, if that was his regular manner or maybe a man saying Help, stop me before it's too late?"

"Look here. I never—"

"My sister Jill—you didn't meet her, did you? She seems flighty, that sensational figure, but she's really a very serious person. She couldn't sleep that whole night. That darling girl, berating herself. Even Cindy. You heard. The whole subject freaks her out." The woman in hiking clothes turned around; Marcia lowered her voice. "Sometimes even I'm convinced we all did something awful. I mean, a man talks to you, and then just that same afternoon . . ."

Celia stood silent.

"Oh, sure, easy to see it now. He really was a spook, that man. But we couldn't imagine it then—Oh, hello, Lexa." Because a woman was standing next to them. "Lexa, such a surprise."

"Marcia, darling, I didn't know you came up here." Lexa was not as tall as Marcia, but she had the same tan skin and bouffant hair, the same air of resolute well-being.

"We don't really. My grandfather lives here—it's his birthday."

"And both of you are here?"

"Oh, sure. Both," Marcia said, though Bernie, Celia saw, was gone. The magazine lay open where he'd left it— "Your Choices of Bait for Trout Fishing"—but his stocky figure in its anomalous business suit had disappeared up the stairs.

"What a break for us. Gregory's at the desk now finding out about our room."

A tall man in tweed slacks and checked shirt, Gregory waved from the desk.

"Such a coincidence," Lexa said. "We were driving

through and the travel guide said Cedar Springs Inn—Greg, look who's here, for God's sake."

Greg expressed pleased surprise.

"A quiet place like this, Greg's been wondering how he could stand it. But now with the two of you here—listen. How about we go out for a drink right now? Drum up a little life."

Marcia said tonight was impossible.

"Tomorrow, then. You know what—if you're here, we'll stay over. We'll find some great restaurant for lunch, and maybe a little antiquing on the way. Remember that time on Long Island when you weren't even looking and you came on that divine old mirror—what was the name of the store again? The Golden Horn."

Marcia said she'd love it but they were tied up with grandfather all day tomorrow.

"So, Greg, we'll stick with the schedule; go tell them, will you?"

She could go too, Celia thought. The session about George Theroux was at an end—no way Marcia was going to revive it. She offered the nod suitable for one who had been of the conversation but not in it, not important enough to have the effusive greetings get interrupted for a dutiful introduction, and in her own room, she went to the phone. "Jason? Jason, am I ever glad you're in. Want to hear what's going on in Cedar Springs?"

"Celia, I'm breathless."

She sat down for her statement. "Thing is, I met those Ellsworths, three of them anyhow, and I don't like them. I don't like them, and what's more, they don't like me."

4

JASON DREW BACK. From the silence that came over the wires, she could see him austerely drawing back. "I didn't mean that," she said quickly. "What I mean is, I don't trust them. That's not right either. I just don't trust anything they say."

"What's the problem?"

"They're very clever. Especially the mother. What a woman at spouting expertise and making it sound natural."

Jason said she could hardly hold cleverness against anyone.

"No. But they're in it together. Whatever *it* is. Oh, I know. That sounds crazy. I just don't—"

"Trust them. Right. Celia—one day—you haven't even been to the police."

She said she was going tomorrow. Lunch time.

"Except for clever people you've turned against at first sight, what's it like there?"

She made a great effort; she was suddenly tired. "Well, the inn is perfect. Right now I'm looking out on this beautiful sloping green that's the town centerpiece. Winding paths and a little white gazebo in the middle. Like a stage set. And the food is divine except they give you too much, and my room's a dream, all chintz and scenic prints and flowered wallpaper. And Professor Ellsworth—Jason, just like you said. He makes a kind of magic out of literature."

"What kind of literature?"

She leaned back in the comfortable chair. "You'd never guess. Not *King Lear* at all, just the opposite. That old man, he said we're going to work on books about children."

"Ah."

"Generalizations today. He explained why there couldn't be any eighteenth-century novels that focused on young people. But there was one marvelous book, he was just going to say which, when—"

"Benjamin Franklin."

"What's that?"

"His autobiography, I bet it's that."

"Jason, why aren't you here instead of me?"

"And if he talks about that, he'll probably take in Gibbon too. His autobiography. You know who he is, Celia, don't you? Wrote *The Decline and Fall of the Roman Empire*," he said before it was necessary for her to prod a recalcitrant memory. "Only two books of the time that give any clue at all to what went on in the adolescent mind. Stupendous, both of them. Family life in those days—an author needed plenty of sly tricks to—Celia, you there?"

"I was just thinking about the Ellsworth family."

"Hey, you have a job too, don't forget," and though his tone was easy, the words reminded her that his main interest was different, had to be different from hers. Oh, he'd keep being supportive, that nice Jason, but the fact was, his reputation was on the line. If she didn't perform well with Professor Ellsworth, his stock with that formidable figure would go down.

All right, she'll be careful. A scrupulous amanuensis and only that, she resolved, when she got into that elderly presence next morning. He was delighted to see her, Professor Ellsworth said. Her tape recorder set? She comfortable in that chair? Now, Celia, you may be surprised at the book we tackle first.

"Benjamin Franklin," she murmured.

"What's that?"

She knew she was blushing. "His autobiography," she mumbled.

The half-closed eyes were turned on her. "I might have known. Someone sent by Jason Bailey would be with me, ahead of me in this project. You're so right, my dear. In an era when it is not permitted to show disrespect to parents, the one book, the only one, in which the strictures are circumvented."

He tugged at the plaid blanket. If you didn't know what was under it, or rather, not under it, you would think he was just an old man unwilling to feel the breeze coming through the window. "So now, what do we have? The opening pages are discreet enough. When the father sends his gifted son to a less worthy school than the boy prefers, when he cuts short all education when the boy is ten and takes him into his candle business, when, finally, he has him bound as an apprentice to brother James when the boy is twelve, in all this we see two strong minds engaged with each other, but in deference to the mandates of the age, we see little more. Young Franklin marches with propriety: a model boy.

"But he is not a model boy. Or rather, that's not all he is, or we would not have this splendid book. So how does that canny manager accomplish his feat? While maintaining the decorum essential for an eighteenth-century son, how does he contrive to show the defiance inevitable for any growing boy? How, in short, does he express what in the seventeen-nineties is inexpressible?"

With just the hint of a foxy smile—watch it, this is where I pull out the rabbit—the lined face turned toward her. "Simple. In dissension with a father surrogate, who is his brother James. 'Differences arise between my Brother and me.' Thus reads an item in one of his working notes. Incidentally, you'll want to check my quotes, my dear, when you come to the final copy. You'll find this one in a brown book with gold letters on the third shelf from the top along that wall. In any case, these differences get the full treatment. When the young apprentice writes something for his brother's newspaper and James fears the boy will get, and I hope I quote correctly, 'too vain'; when the young apprentice decides that his brother's insistence on hard work demeans him; when the insistence modulates into beatings which, though standard for that time as between master and apprentice, the latter takes, and I quote again, 'extremely amiss.' And finally when, after five years and much anger, young Benjamin, though he has just signed new indentures, nevertheless plays out one of the great scenes of American myth by deciding he will assert his freedom and leave. Are you tired, Celia my dear?"

Tired! She's enthralled. Impossible to think he can't see, he can't walk, that all this has been stored inside him, waiting for the mechanical aid of a tape recorder to take it down. She wants it to go on and on, that fluent voice cutting through two centuries to get at adolescent obstinacy and tenacity and pride. "Thrilling," she said.

"I have to think about where we go next."

"How about Gibbon?"

The watery eyes squinted, the creased neck jolted up. "Say that again."

"Gibbon's autobiography," her voice said.

"Well, well. I'd clean forgotten. Celia, how clever of you."

Is it right to stand here, preening herself, accepting his praise? Should she confess that until last night she hardly knew who Gibbon was?

"Just because he's English, for me to forget. The only other book that tells the story the child culture of their time forbids them to tell, which is the shaking off by a child of paternal dominance. Well, I have to consider a little." He was considering now, such a long silence she decided he would produce it on the spot, another effortless evocation. But he said finally he needed time, they'd talk about it this afternoon. Meanwhile, had she met his family?

She said she'd seen them in the hotel dining room.

"Marcia and Bernard you met here, of course. I'll tell them all to introduce themselves."

She's ingratiated herself: Celia, the literature scholar.

"Marcia's brother Jerry is some years younger. Twenty-eight, I'd say. Possibly twenty-seven. A fine young man. For a couple of years he couldn't decide which of his undoubted talents to focus on, but now he's settled on engineering, he's going ahead like a house afire. Then there's Gillian. Bright as a whistle, that one. A merchandise expert, I forget which store. And the youngest. Cindy. A math wiz. Last time her mother came she read me one of Cindy's articles. I couldn't understand a word. Imagine, those abstruse concepts out of the head of a seventeen-year-old girl. Oh, and her mother. Madeleine, lovely competent woman. When my son died two years ago she held the family together. Have I bored you, my dear? Oh, you're sweet to say so. A grandfather's privilege, you know, to keep in touch. Privilege and also, I like to think, duty. Well, you run along. On the way out, tell Les he can come up now."

Les was his attendant, from what she could make out, his only one, a red-cheeked young man already standing expectant at the end of the hall. He smiled when he saw her and said she was doing a good job with the professor.

"How do you know?"

"I know he was in a good mood when he knew you were coming. Chipper." Les talked with the mild twang that said farm boy, that said country.

"Isn't he always chipper when people are coming?"

Les looked up and down the hall. "Not exactly," he said and closed his lips with an intimation of disapproval.

So he doesn't like that family either. Or maybe doesn't trust them. Or maybe I'm just projecting on him the feelings I'd be more comfortable if someone else were sharing. Me and Les in subversive cahoots.

A cough from down the hall—he'd better go in, she said. No, wait a minute. Could he tell her where the police station was?

"Well, sure. That big red building on Woodley, southwest corner of the green. You can't miss it—there's a sporting goods store, Victory, on the first floor. The police are one flight up."

She didn't miss. A walk along the road where every rise provided a memorable vista, a stop to admire the green and its resident gazebo in daylight, then up the stairs to the room where the man behind the desk told her the one she wanted to see was Officer Hurley. Out to lunch right now. Sit there, Miss.

She sat on the designated bench. She'd put in her time in big-city police stations; who that has ever jumped to a mugger's warning or lost a wallet or come home to find the front door unlatched hasn't? But evidently police can function in quarters like this too, places where there is less acrimonious bustle than she'd noted in the sporting goods store downstairs. Well, what would you expect for a town where the only disasters are a bicycle stolen, or a car gone off the road into the soft shoulder, or maybe—dire event—someone's cat up a tree? Unless you count a man found shot behind the inn, and from what she has so far seen, no one's counting.

She might have known: in such a town, of course the chief officer would be out at lunch time. He probably goes home where his wife has a hot meal for him and the two small boys; after it, there's time for a game of catch on the front lawn. Forty-five minutes, at least.

But in fact it was only fifteen minutes before Officer Hurley appeared and asked her to come inside. He led her into a room even quieter than the front one; then he leaned back—a heavy-set man with Les's ruddy coloring on a square face—and said he was wondering when she would show up.

"So you know who I am."

"We're a small town, Miss Sommerville." As if she doesn't know. "Besides, when a guest at the inn has been found dead and two days later the woman who was engaged to him turns up, and when it also appears that she's going to be around for a while working for Professor Ellsworth . . ." Like a conjurer, he put out his hands: no secrets.

She took a deep breath. "Then you are conducting an investigation."

One of the hands reached for a pencil on the desk. "Some troubling questions about any violent death. Sure, we investigate."

"But you told everyone it was suicide."

"What we said was lots of the signs pointed to suicide." The square face held no expression, but somewhere along the line his tone had sharpened. "That's still true. A dead man with a gun in his hand and a chest wound that could be self-inflicted points to suicide. It's what I told the newspapers, what I told people at your college, also what I told Mr. Theroux's brother when we released the body to him yesterday morning."

She turned for a minute toward the window. A single car, the only activity outside the Cedar Springs police station. "So this investigation, what'd you find out about George Theroux?"

"Only what you yourself doubtless know. According to police in his own city, he had no enemies, he wasn't involved in any feuds, there's no indication that he felt any need to take precautions. But he'd had a bad shock the day before his death when his engagement was broken. He told

44

all his friends he was devastated. The bottom had fallen out, was what a couple of them said."

"Want me to tell you something you didn't find out?" Her own voice sounded heavy, combative, after Hurley's neutral one. "George didn't commit suicide. Never, never—you didn't know him or you'd agree. Such a steady, strong, confident man—he wouldn't go in for something so desperate, so, I don't know, disorderly. Besides, he was a stoic. That was one of his beliefs, his big outspoken beliefs. You should accept suffering, put up a quiet fight against it. Suicide isn't a quiet fight, it's a dashing statement. And besides all that"—still too loud, but she went on—"besides, he didn't have the imagination, he wasn't even that impulsive. Not impulsive in the least. He'd never lunge into action. He only did things that had been planned long in advance, things that were practical and logical and neat."

"Miss Sommerville, four years ago I had a colleague. Practical, strong, confident—what was it you said? Yes. Unimaginative. Stoic. That too. On a Sunday night he found out his wife was having an affair. On Monday he hired a boat, rowed out to the middle of a lake, put rocks in his pockets and jumped."

"A wife," she said. "The poor man was crazy with grief. It wasn't like that with George and me."

"You mean, he was the one to break the engagement?"

She was surprised at the sudden flare-up within her of objection. Vanity, vanity. "No, I did, you heard right about that. But look—you have to understand George. His passion wasn't really for me, it was for arrangements. And once he decided I was the woman for him, the arrangements naturally revolved around me. Sure, the bottom fell out— out of his precious schedule. Men don't kill themselves for a disarranged schedule." Talking about George brought him back; she pictured him standing next to her, the anxious, pompous face nodding, approving. What you're saying is exactly right, Celia dear.

"Besides, there's something I bet your investigation didn't tell you. He didn't come here for a tug at the old school ties. This was a trip to get him money."

Hurley's eyebrows went up. "Is that what Mr. Theroux told you? He was coming to Cedar Springs to get money?"

"He told me indirectly. There was this house he wanted to buy. Talk about passion, he did have one after all. A passion for a house he couldn't afford. But what he said was, after his visit with the Ellsworth family, maybe then he would be able to afford it."

So what was her idea? Hurley put down the pencil.

"We're talking about a family with money. Big money. At least, money they can someday expect—isn't that the accepted wisdom? So suppose George knew some way to diminish those expectations if they didn't fork over?"

"Just as likely to think he planned to borrow from the professor," Hurley said. "He'd gone to school, as I understand, with Roy Ellsworth. Maybe he figured he could exploit that relationship, work on the old man's sympathy."

"George would never borrow. It's almost as unlikely as suicide. Borrowing—it means to strike an imbalance. George, the math professor—with him everything had to come out equal. Before he put down money for anything, he had a mental image of the sum on deposit that was going to cover it."

Hurley allowed himself a quick smile. "So that leaves blackmail. Some species of blackmail—that your idea?" He didn't wait for her eager nod. "You can't have it both ways, Miss Sommerville. You say he didn't have the imagination, the daring for something as untidy as suicide. But blackmail works out to just about the most undignified, untidy act there is."

Touché. Lulled by her own certitudes, she'd walked right

into it. "So if it was suicide, why pack a suitcase and drive three hours and register at an inn he didn't know?"

"I said there were some questions," Hurley nicely admitted. "One theory is that he visited his old school, and the memories activated whatever pain he was carrying around."

"What'd he do at the school?"

"Just walked about."

"Who'd he talk to?"

When the phone rang, Hurley told someone he wouldn't be available for another ten minutes. Putting her on notice. "No one. There's still a teacher from his era who lives there. A Mr. Druer. Elias Druer. But Mr. Theroux didn't try to contact him. He was seen standing in front of the library; others spotted him walking around the gym."

Eighty-five steps and two left turns to the gym. She said George never even had a gun, but Hurley didn't dignify that with an answer. Unfair. There he sits, with his mild square undemonstrative face, and he blocks her at every turn. She's making sense, she's drawing on insights sharpened by months and months of intimacy, and she's getting nowhere. Stymied.

"Could I ask you something? Do you know what that family were doing at the time George was supposedly shooting himself?"

"You mean, do they have alibis?" Indulging her, he drawled it out. Alibi: that word susceptible of parody, of fraud, of conniving misuse. "Actually, all of them were moseying around, in and out of their rooms, the way people will mosey around at a hotel on a cloudy afternoon. Well, not quite all. Mrs. Ellsworth was playing bridge in the lobby; she never got up between one and four, which is the critical time. And the son, Jerry, was climbing a mountain."

"You sure about that?"

A quick glance from across the desk. "No one saw him or went with him, if that's what you're asking."

She pictured that sallow face: the thin lips, the languid gaze. "Is that something he regularly does, go mountain climbing?"

"Our Vermont air is supposed to be invigorating." Hurley had the grace to give a small defensive cough. "They tell me it rouses people to feats they wouldn't ordinarily go in for."

She heard her tense voice. "Okay. So four of them could have done it." Is she including Cindy? A seventeen-year-old in a high-school sweatshirt? Yes, she's including Cindy. "Four," she repeated. "Doesn't that figure in your investigation?"

For the first time, he gave a reproachful sigh. "You know what you haven't mentioned, Miss Sommerville. A motive. From where I'm sitting, there is none. No reason the Ellsworths could have had for killing an old school friend of their father's."

"How about the motive we discussed before? Blackmail. George knew something about them, let's say something he'd heard from their father before he died, and he threatened to tell the professor. I mean, the professor thinks they're such shining specimens, he keeps saying it, it's obviously his main concern. But suppose he found out different?"

"You mean, then he wouldn't leave them all his considerable amounts of money?"

Exactly what she means.

"It's a neat idea, Miss Sommerville. The only thing is, we haven't the slightest clue there's anything to blackmail them for. In which case, the opposite proposition is equally plausible."

"What's that?"

"That if they killed someone, that's something Grandpa

wouldn't like. Wouldn't like at all, he'd make sure they got their hands on none of his money. According to which, Miss Sommerville"—Hurley spoke in the brisk tone that was at once summation and dismissal—"you might conclude that the Ellsworth family has a very strong motive to not go killing anyone."

5

"CELIA, WANT SOME of this gravy?"

"Yes, please."

"You should try these rolls. Specialty of the house."

"Maybe later, thanks."

"This Vermont weather, does great things to your appetite, don't you find?"

"Oh, it surely does."

"Such wonderful air. Even lets you sleep better."

She was at their table, part of the family. They had insisted. Primed for action, ready for concerted good will, they had looked over as soon as she came into the dining room. She was to move right to their table, no, not too much trouble at all, Emmy Lou would set another place, yes, plenty of room. They were firm about it; firm but not conspicuously pleased; plainly, the professor had been at them. So here she was, recipient of unwilling Ellsworth courtesy: her reward for having known about Edward Gibbon.

But she didn't know any more about them. Oh, she could sort them out; that was something. Mrs. Ellsworth, whose gaze seemed activated, even while she was eating, to take in everyone at once, and Marcia, of course, with Bernie still in an inappropriate suit, and the sallow Jerry, who didn't go at his food with the heartiness of the others, and

Jill, whose figure, as spectacular as promised, was set off by a black-and-yellow sweater and black pants, and Cindy, still robust and abstractedly sullen in her sweatshirt. But though she'd been with them almost an hour, while the murmur of talk went on and the efficient Emmy Lou replaced the fruit cup with cold soup and took that away in turn for steaming platters of meat and vegetables and potatoes, she had found out only that the murmur was less animated with her here. Celia, the outsider. Party pooper. Because surely they didn't sound like this, all clipped and constrained, when she looked over from her own table and marveled at that free-wheeling jollity.

"Hope my grandfather isn't working you too hard." Marcia, in an obvious effort to be polite.

"But I love it, it's such great stuff. All about children in literature."

"Children. That's funny," Jill said.

"Actually, when you think about it, not so funny," Marcia after a second pointed out. Heads nodded, eyes shifted sideways, Celia was conscious of a communal thought making its way around the table.

"It was Gibbon this afternoon," she said—will that help out? "You know, Edward Gibbon. Explaining what a time he had. Because in those days, seventeen-eighties, no one could admit to rebelling against parents. And so it's fascinating to see how he gets around the rules and gives us his own kind of rebellion, even though you have to read between the lines to find it."

They weren't listening; she had lost them; Gibbon after all was going to be no help. But though across from her an argument had started about which of the luscious desserts to favor, it was Professor Ellsworth she heard, the aged and occasionally cracked voice rolling out the smooth sentences. "Not an overt defiance, as with Franklin; it's his body, rather, that defies Father. Because the fact is that it was through sickness that young Gibbon achieved control of his life. Bouts of ill health got him what he wanted. Every time his father sent him to one or another of the schools he detested, he developed morbid signs of illness. And every time he stayed home, with an assiduous tutor or a loving aunt but in any case covered by the one-to-one supervision which his nature craved, and doing the independent study which was, indeed, to prove optimal preparation for his great work, that accommodating body left him in peace."

"Fascinating," she repeated, and saw the relief: she was not going to belabor them with Gibbon. She would not even—she made a quick decision—repeat what he'd said about Cindy: "That alert mind—school brings out the best there is, a girl who gets a real charge from amiable competition." They don't want to hear about alert minds, even of one of their own; they would rather listen to Bernie. Or, rather, not listen; Bernie's flat voice called for minimal attention. He was talking about Vermont. Population over half a million. Almost all of them—wait a minute, he has it here in his notebook—yes; 96 percent, to be exact, born in the United States. Sixty-seven percent of these born in Vermont. Only 1 percent nonwhite, which is a record for the nation.

They all nodded, over bites of salad. They didn't interrupt, but they were not enthralled either. What they were, she saw, was glad to have him talk. He absolved them: they didn't have to make conversation with the newcomer. In place of the casual hilarity that maintained when she wasn't there, it was convenient to have the eager pedantry dispensed by Bernie.

"Unemployment a couple of years ago less than five percent. Not too bad. Number of those in rural areas—hold it, I know I wrote it down"—another search through the notebook, which this evening he has drawn from the pocket of a gray pin-striped suit—"Here: sixty percent. That's high. Makes it just about the most rural state in the nation. Tallest mountain—"

"That the one you climbed, Jerry? The tallest?" Cindy said.

An instant's agitation, while they adjusted to the change of topic, or maybe to the change to this particular topic. But Jerry's languid voice went smoothly on. "She's real proud of me," he told Celia. "Even though I didn't take the most difficult trail. Not the eensy baby one but not the most difficult either. The moderate—it's listed in the pamphlet out there."

"Next time take the difficult," Cindy said.

"Sure. Me with three chocolate bars and an extra sweater, on that trail that calls for rock climbing. Thanks."

Celia put down her fork. When had he done this feat, she asked.

"Three days ago."

"You should have taken me," Cindy said. "Then I wouldn't have been around when that spooky man shot himself."

"What's it like, climbing around here?" Celia said.

"You want the details?—Jill, shut up. Just because you heard it doesn't mean someone else. Well, so I left at one. One on the button. Say half an hour's walk to the starting point, that's when I bought the chocolate bars." He leaned back to let Emmy Lou take his plate, which was still half-full. Chocolate bars, that's for him, Celia thought. Junk food. Anything that can be grabbed at a run, held in a careless hand, eaten in quick disarray at a counter. "Then I started up. Easy going for a while, the hard part didn't start till I went over some fallen trees and up on a kind of ridge. That was a bummer. Stones, rocks, roots, water, mud, a real mess. Once I dislodged a rock, it went clattering down, I thought I was going with it. But I didn't." A rueful smile on the sallow face: Here I am, folks. "Then it got easier again. Not real easy, just a decent path. Lots of pine needles, so I lay down, I think I went to sleep. I tell you how long I slept?" He turned to Bernie: man of facts. "Half an hour, maybe. I ate the chocolate bars, all three of them. Dumb, don't tell me—what if you break a leg? But great news, I didn't break a leg."

He didn't see anyone either. Or, rather, no one saw him: Officer Hurley. Celia took the last bite of salad.

"My brother, the mountain goat," Jill said.

Another aborted smile from Jerry. He'd take her sometime, he told Celia.

She thanked him.

"Today would've been a great day. Not too much sun, little wind."

"She couldn't have gone today," Cindy said.

"I know. She works for Grandpa."

"Not just that. Lunch time she went to the police station. We saw her, Jill and I. Jill, didn't we? We were across the street at Jefferson's buying sunglasses." The adolescent face serenely met their stares. Had Jill already told the others? Had there been a concerted decision not to divulge this, and was Cindy deliberately making trouble? Did they not want her to know they were making it their business to know about her? "The municipal building, anyhow," Cindy went on. "Unless she was going to the water department. Or sanitation. They're all in there."

"Hope it isn't any problem," Madeleine Ellsworth said.

She was conscious of the scrutiny of five pairs of eyes. She had some question about her car, she said. That is, about the registration. That is, about insurance if she was living for a month in another state.

"Any problems I'd be glad to help you," Jerry said.

She thanked him.

"Or if your own car is out of commission and you want to go someplace, we have two cars just sitting there."

Another thanks.

"Well, so long as no real problem," Madeleine Ellsworth said. "Not like our other Boston guest."

A second to catch her breath while she realized what guest was meant. "I hope not."

"Now you mention it, some rotten trick that man pulled." Jerry spoke with sudden fierceness. Maybe it's a family trait: the ability to abruptly shift conversational gears. "Treating my sisters like that," he said.

Celia stared at the three resplendent, sated faces.

"Oh, sure, I understand, if you're going to commit suicide, you're excused from thinking, you've hit bottom, how can you feel for anyone else—all that. But still, the way he did it was disgusting."

"Jerry, relax," Marcia said.

"Listen. I read last month about this guy who killed himself by jumping from a thirty-story building. Only in the process he landed on a twenty-two-year-old man who was walking by. Well, okay. Theroux wasn't as bad as that, you might say. But in a way he was. Look how he goes about it. First he announces that he's our father's old friend, so we'll all pay attention to him, he gets our sympathy. Then he works up this conversation about how interested in us he is, he can't wait to find out what we're doing, how's our life, etcetera, etcetera. Then a little song and dance about Grandpa. Then he takes his gun and sashays out. Well, if that isn't landing on us, I don't know what is. No, I'll skip dessert. Okay, the blueberry pie," his voice allowed to Marcia, who passed on the word to Emmy Lou.

"Then where he does it. What a frost. One of the few decent things about suicide is it's private. You're on your own. No big messes for someone else. It's you and your gun, behind locked doors. Or your pills or your rope or whatever. You don't tell anyone beforehand or they'd have to stop you. Right? Ditto asking for help with the arrangements. What gives it the zing. Solo performance." Jerry's aggrieved stare made a tour of the table.

"So what place does this Theroux fellow pick? Right

down by the brook where anyone who's got an urge for peaceful scenery is going to go. I saw Cindy and one of her new boyfriends—Cindy, don't blush, they're not bad kids—I saw them heading down there right that morning. So suppose she'd gone a couple of hours later, she'd been the one to find him. A seventeen-year-old girl coming on a man with a hole in his chest."

The seventeen-year-old girl looked with pointed modesty at the tablecloth.

"You almost think he had it in for us. Some old grudge. Maybe Dad didn't pay him enough attention or invite him some time when he wanted to be invited or answer one of the phone calls—something. Those old-boy friendships, they look jolly but there can be some nasty feelings underneath. So anyhow, he thinks, I'll fix them, I'll make it as miserable for them as I can. If I'm going to knock myself off I'll do it where they have to suffer."

"Jerry, that's dumb," Marcia said.

"And another thing," the critique went imperturbably on. "We're not supposed to let on to my grandfather. We just sit and don't mention it, so when he talks about his son Roy and his pal George, when he gets started on that bit like he did yesterday, we have to clam up. Regular zombies. Well, I understand the reason and all that, but look what it does to us. I sit there shivering: Jesus, if a newspaper reporter accidentally gets in or Lester makes a break or even me. If I forget and say the wrong thing. He might have a heart attack. And this is supposed to be a vacation. Big laugh."

"Jerry, calm down."

"I mean it. Why'd that man have to come here anyhow? If he was so gung ho to shoot himself, why not like a gentleman in his own bedroom!"

"Jerry, we have a guest at the table, did you forget?" Mrs. Ellsworth's gaze went meaningfully down the table. "The way you carry on, Celia will think you're blaming her. And it's not her fault, heavens knows, that some wretched man decides to come to Cedar Springs and commit suicide."

6

"SO CELIA, HERE we go." Ten in the morning, and from the open window a breeze lifted the fringed edge of the professor's blanket. "Middle of the nineteenth century, and children have made it. They are recognizable creatures in the collective mind, which means they are ready to make their debut in fiction. A glum debut, to be sure; it's the short end of the stick that is put into the small outstretched hand. Oliver Twist makes it out of the poorhouse to wind up a captive of the underworld. Little Nell lives alone with Grandpa in a world bent on doing them in. David Copperfield acts out the original of Life with Stepfather. Florence Dombey is given to understand by her father that daughter is a dirty word. As for Jane Eyre—my dear, do you feel a draft?"

"I'll just close this window a little," she said.

"So for all the cozy ring of the new set of rights, the fact remains that a paragon is still what the authorities require. Disobedience in childhood works out to depravity in adulthood: this is the basic equation and the primal fear. So we see why, in those early books, dutifulness, courage, faith and above all obedience light up the sweet and usually frail little face. As for jealousy, resentment, irritability, meanness, those traits that future generations will assign as the normal paraphernalia of the child, in eighteen-fifty they

57

have not yet been accredited, which gives the novelist no right to use them . . ." Another pause, this time for a sly gleam in the wrinkled eyes. "Standard childish malfeasance not yet accredited, which means no vocabulary for it—I have to laugh. If there'd been no vocabulary for describing my grandson Jerry we'd have been lost. That boy—bois-terous, hyperactive, uncontrolled, aggressive, all these terms served for him. Let the books name it, Jerry exhibited it. And I must admit, his parents weren't happy. I told them not to worry. 'Inside that odious little hellion,' I said, 'is a fundamental sweetness and goodness.' Yes. Just what I said. And of course I was right, events have borne me out, that exemplary character he is today. . . . Celia, a little tired this morning. We'll move on more quickly this afternoon."

She went down to the kitchen, where Lester was taking a chicken out of the oven. "Is he all right?"

"Why not?"

"He quit early. Not like him. He usually goes on till his voice gets hoarse."

"That family tires him out. He says he likes to have them"—Lester kept his gaze on the steaming bird—"but they tire him out."

She watched him, cutting, seasoning, slicing, moving adroitly around the kitchen. With his ruddy cheeks, curly hair, bright eyes he looked as if he might be perched on a tractor in an ad for farm implements or perhaps a new brand of jeans, but what he was doing was fixing an ap-petizing tray for lunch. "Where'd you learn all that?"

"My father taught us. My brother Arnie and me. My mother died when I was eight. It was learn to cook or live on corn flakes. Some day, Arnie and I, we'll open our own restaurant."

Meanwhile he's taking first-rate care of an elderly man who could afford a retinue of servants but obviously prefers a single young and cheerful one. She watched another min-

58

ute—sautéed string beans next to the chicken—then she asked if he knew where the Cedar Springs Prep School was.

"You know where Main Street veers off right there beyond the inn? Follow the signs to the horse farm, then left about a mile to the covered bridge—you haven't seen it yet? you'll love it—then right to Brookdale and keep straight. You thinking of going there?"

"Sort of."

"Good five miles each way."

She had a car at the inn, she told him. It was just, this beautiful road, she liked walking over.

"Three miles north on Brookdale and you'll see the gate posts. Big stone ones." Les concentrated on folding a napkin. "That school—isn't it the place that man went to? The one who had that bad accident a couple of days ago, only we're not supposed to mention it to the professor."

Bad accident: such delicacy. He can't possibly know her thoughts, but some instinct leads him to put things the right way. Now he looked warily around, though this bright kitchen was on the other side of the house from that upstairs bedroom, no chance of sound carrying. "You know what? He wouldn't mind. He wants to hear what's going on. Sure, he's a brain, his books are number one, but he has me read him the paper every day too. That's his thing, to be up on what's going on." The ruddy face turned toward the staircase. "You know what he would mind? If he figured we were holding out on him, that would give him a heart attack sure enough. He can have his secrets, but watch out if he thinks you're keeping secrets from him."

Oh, she likes this young man who has discerned the innate suspiciousness of invalidism. More, she senses an affinity between them. Not only is there that mistrust of the family that is based on nothing verifiable; they both see Professor Ellsworth the same way: someone dedicated, gifted, scholarly, capable of great feats of memory and application, but also foxy, furtive, troubled, harboring obscure motivations and undecipherable thoughts.

Was she serious about driving out to the school, Les went on. She should be careful of those speeding cars. Also, just before the covered bridge, she might want to look on the left. Where route 84A crosses over. Small red house, oversize red barn sort of in a hollow. That belongs to them. His family. The barn doesn't serve for anything special, time is gone when you can make a living from dairy cows, and besides, his father's health is not all Arnie and he would like it to be. But they're attached to the old place. They think it is pretty damn good.

She thought it was good too, though the honking behind didn't give her much time for looking. Careful of those speeding cars? Les wasn't kidding. Some with drivers who seemed to be twelve years old as they zoomed up and down the hills but must, she knew, have passed their sixteenth birthday. And some—one anyhow—with a driver who looked familiar. The red car that passed when she was at the bridge and then again, going slowly the other way, as she approached the stone gates—was that Jerry behind the wheel?

It signifies nothing. He can be out for an aimless drive. He can think she is out for an aimless drive. It doesn't mean he's checking up on her. Anyhow, she's certainly checking on them—why shouldn't they do the same to her, she thought, as she turned into the driveway George had said he could navigate blindfolded.

Some very young boys were playing on a field to the left—summer camp?—but she went straight ahead, where two men in shorts and sweat shirts were standing. Mr. Druer? Anyone know where she can find Mr. Druer? They shook their heads. Sorry. Never heard of him—why doesn't she try the office? That building, first door as she comes in, she'll see the sign.

The sign was there, but the young man behind a desk

didn't know either. Druer? Elias Druer? One of the new counselors, maybe? Someone working on that renovation at the dorm? Well, then, would he by any chance be the new chef?

"I think he must be, um, sort of old," she said.

"Stan, you know someone old? Druer?" Because another man had come in. Stan heard the problem and nodded. Elias Druer. Sure thing. Follow me.

She followed him along well-kept paths and past imposing stone buildings, which grew less imposing as the tour proceeded; the place where her guide stopped was a three-story house with a trellised porch, crumbling paint, and a sign that said PROCEED AT OWN RISK. She shouldn't worry about this last, her guide said. It was just to keep out the boys. The building was not now used—except by Mr. Druer, of course. He was on the third floor—could she make her way alone?

She had to make her way up only one flight; then a voice called down. "You the one who called? Miss Sommerville? Wait there, I'll be along."

Even older than she expected, the bent figure carrying a cane that materialized from the dim stairway. But his voice was firm. "Miss Sommerville? Good to see you. I'd ask you to come up but the place isn't geared for entertaining. So we'll go down, me first, if you please. If I fall I don't want to encumber you."

He didn't fall, though there was much clutching of banister and adjusting of cane on steps till he reached the bottom. They could sit in here, he said: a room that went the whole length of the house. In his day they called it the Rec Room, which covered a multitude of jolly purposes. Plays. Debates. Square dances. Indoor picnics. Now there was a building for each of these: the age of specialization. Well, that was not the only change. Now, Miss Sommerville, what can I do for you?

She shifted on the bench which, with a matching table,

was the only furniture. Uncomfortable for her, must be worse for him. But he laid the cane on the floor, folded his hands in front of him, and sat with a benign look as she put her question. She wondered if he remembered far back, forty or so years back, actually, when Roy Ellsworth and George Theroux were students.

"Roy Ellsworth. Didn't I hear that he died, couple of years back? Funny. They're such kids when you're telling them to sit up straight in class, then they go dying ahead of you."

Wearing the gratified triumph of a survivor, he leaned further across the table. "The school was different then. My father started it. Seventy years ago, can you tie that! When he died it was mine but I didn't want it. No talent for running things. No drive. I sold it, with two provisos, to this smart young couple. I'd keep teaching till age sixty, and I'd have living quarters here in perpetuity. I used to have a place down the road—pretty house with red shutters and tile roof next to the pond, maybe you noticed it. But then they needed it for an infirmary so they moved me here." He gestured upward, that gabled place to which he climbs with effort and in which he has no room for entertaining. Well, it's in perpetuity, there's that.

"What a school when my father ran it. Different, did I say? Another world. I'm talking seventy years ago, mind. Freedom, that was the big thing. Freedom for schoolboys, can you tie that. Walk around any morning, and some boys were working their heads off in the chemistry lab, but some were sitting out all day on the lawn. Their choice. No pressure, no coercion. One boy never learned to read till he was sixteen—that was the story, anyhow—then he learned in a big rush because there was a manual about tools and he needed it to finish some job. Well, you get the idea. If they turned out to be truck drivers, that was okay. Just so they were happy truck drivers."

Mr. Druer slid his elbows across the table. "And sex,

what a blast. Openness, my father said. Tolerance. Self-expression. Children will never be cruel unless they have been forced to suppress some strong emotion: Emmanuel Druer. It's all in his book, out of print but you can still find a copy. One boy kept setting fires; one night we all nearly blew up. My father explained to his parents what was wrong. They repressed him. They built up his fears about sex. They didn't have the proper heart-to-hearts. They didn't encourage openness by walking around naked. Much walking around naked in our house when I was growing up. Mother, father, big sister, me. All that bobbing and bouncing, what a show. Then the rules changed. Clothes back on, breasts and bottoms covered up. New regime." He looked upward to the ceiling, where the beams crossed and recrossed; his gaze, like his memory, was most comfortable focusing on something distant.

Mr. Druer rearranged his legs under the table. "Happy truck drivers. They better not graduate any like that today. The school wouldn't last a second. They have to toe the line, this crowd. Cut their hair just so and get on time to chapel and hole up in the dorms by ten and get good marks. Good marks so they'll be a cinch for the best colleges. Factory for successful preppies.

"But you know what?" The watery gaze turned down from the ceiling. "My father would've had a good laugh. If you don't give 'em freedom, they'll take it by stealth, he used to say. Pompous old fellow, but he had it right. I hear them in the woods over there. One of them sneaking in with a girl, then another couple, then another. Or sometimes three of them with the same girl, can't say I like that so much. Or I hear things. Even up here, I hear what goes on down at the main building. One of those big successes booted out for selling coke. Another for stealing exams. Can you tie that! My father didn't make them take exams, these kids figure it pays to steal them."

Try again. "Mr. Druer, I wonder if you remember Roy Ellsworth or George Theroux."

"Bunch of mixed-up kids. Role confusion, we called it then. They didn't know who they were. Those years, they cut their hair short. Crew cuts . . . book bags . . . football letters . . ." He was mumbling, delving without success into the pool of memories. "Ego identity . . ." His eyes were glazed, as if seeing faces in all the yearbooks massed together, one page after the other.

"George Theroux," she said.

The gnarled hands turned over. "Didn't I read about him in the paper the other day? Some accident. Yes. Suicide, they thought. Funny thing, George committing suicide. If anyone, I'd have thought Roy would be the one."

"Why is that?" she said to the suddenly alert eyes, the slyly knowing voice: the pool has netted something after all.

"Roy was the problem. Real perverse kid, that one."

"Like what?" Let him keep talking, let him keep talking.

"He didn't want contact with his father. Wouldn't see him, wouldn't talk to him. Well, lots of them turn hostile. They hit fifteen, sixteen, Daddy is suddenly the enemy. But not like this kid. He took it to extremes. Paranoia, almost. Like when it came to Father, something snapped inside." He was fading out again.

"Roy didn't like his father? Professor Ellsworth?" Will the name do it, give him something to hang the details on? "Besides, it was just the two of them—didn't the step-mother die when Roy was ten?"

"Two of them," Mr. Druer repeated and slid his elbows further along the table.

"They lived in Boston," she prodded.

"Boston. Yes." The gaze grew less bleary: Boston, the catalyst. "He wouldn't go home for Christmas vacation. Everyone goes home. Every single boy. There's only a jan-itor on hand. And me," the morose voice added.

"Maybe his father was going someplace. A trip."

"No. Roy didn't want to be with him, that was all."

"Is that what he said?"

"He never said anything. They didn't want him to be alone so I moved into the dorm, but he never said anything." Mr. Druer rubbed his eyes. "I was a physics teacher. Kids don't talk to the physics teacher."

"Look. You sure about this?"

"Roy wouldn't take presents from him either," the voice went doggedly on. "Any present his father sent, Roy threw it away. Some skis came while I was there. Plenty of snow up here in winter, all the kids need skis. Roy took them and put them outside; they stayed there till some other boy walked off with them."

"Maybe they had a fight, just those few weeks. You said yourself—"

"One year Roy didn't go home for eighteen months. Don't ask me how he managed, a fifteen-year-old boy on his own. Just we all knew he didn't go home." Mr. Druer was on track now, a front-row seat at that distant time. "And did no good for Ellsworth to come here. One day in spring he came to take Roy out to lunch. They all like an outing for lunch. Get away from the institutional food. Back then they went to that place the other side of town. Paddy's—I hear it's still there. So that day I was passing when his father sat there, and Roy wouldn't get into the car, wouldn't talk, wouldn't explain. Wouldn't."

When Mr. Druer's voice wound down, she heard that other voice dictating into a tape machine. What makes children act the way they do? How much can you blame on parents? How much can parents blame on the mandates of the time?

"Well, listen. Didn't you have guidance counselors in those days? Deans? People to talk to a troubled kid?"

"Sure, we had 'em. Forty years ago, you think that was ancient times." For an instant he looked imperious, this denizen in perpetuity of the Cedar Springs Preparatory

School who was not known to people at the office. "Everyone worried. Other pupils had problems with parents, sure they did, but nothing that went on so long or made such complications or involved such strong feelings. A situation like that, it's a bad mark against a school. They used to have meetings to talk about him, then they'd report to us teachers. It's not good, it's not natural, wrack your brains, tell us anything that might be helpful to our understanding. No one could help. No one understood. He didn't stand out, after all, in any other way. Wasn't one of the whiz kids, but not a deadbeat either. It was baffling. Roy Ellsworth, the one nut Cedar Springs Prep School couldn't crack."

"How about the father? A professor, after all—what was his explanation?"

"He was as baffled as the rest of them. Baffled, heartsick, angry." Mr. Druer let his head slump further on his elbows. "Once they even called his friend in. What'd you say his name was? George. Tall uptight boy—I gave him an A in physics, but I can't say I liked him. Highly unusual, asking one pupil to spill the beans about another, but they were desperate. They talked to him man to man. George, of course you want to help your friend, if you know anything, great responsibility, bad situation, and so on and so on. It got them no place. He just stood there. You know that stubborn look they get when they clam up."

Yes, she knows that look. George, were you privy to some information about your friend Roy, some great disclosure, and did you carry it around all these years in that uptight, methodical, pompous head? And is it connected with the reason you came here three days ago to talk to a family you'd never met, the reason you're dead now in a disaster for which everyone blames me?

"Did you ever talk to either of them after they left school? Roy or George, I mean. Or hear anything? Mr. Druer?" It was useless; she knew it was useless as soon as she saw the white head slump the rest of the way on the bent elbows. "Role confusion," Mr. Druer said. "Ego identity," his voice mumbled, and they were back with the crew haircuts, the book bags, the group snapshots, all doing their routine job of concealing the undifferentiated adolescent traumas.

7

"IT WAS A MESS," she said to Jason that night on the phone. "One of those mean situations adolescence can let you in for. Principals miserable. Authorities helpless. Onlookers purposefully indifferent."

She had wanted to talk to Jason, but she was also reluctant to call him: on her third day, to seem to be taking for granted they had an established ritual. But as she came to her room after dinner, the phone was ringing. Where'd she been? Why'd she take so long downstairs? Didn't she understand how anxious he was to hear?

He listened without comment to her account of Roy at school, then he said that animosity between parent, especially a single parent, and adolescent child wasn't so unusual. It was what kept the prep schools in business, the best thing they had going for them. "If things were hunky-dory over the breakfast table, those mixed-up kids could go off every morning to the high school half a mile from their own house."

"This was different. Your average mixed-up kid doesn't stay away from home for a year and a half. Or refuse any communication at all. I mean, they may think they hate Daddy, but if he sends them a pair of much-needed skis, they're perfectly willing to slide downhill on them."

"And no one had any idea what caused this?"

"Not a clue."

"Rotten for Professor Ellsworth. That proud man, to have to face all that sympathy and curiosity. The legitimatized prying."

She gripped the receiver. Hearing Mr. Druer's rambling voice go on, she had thought of this from the standpoint of Roy. Roy and of course his best chum George, who had stood stolid and uncommunicative when the school authorities tried to interrogate him. But now she realized the same interrogation must have been mandated for the problem father. Professor Ellsworth, is there anything in the past that might have incited this strong reaction? Please believe, Professor Ellsworth, that we're anxious to help you. Maybe, Professor Ellsworth, if we all sit down together and go over the evidence once again. . . .

"Jason, another thing. No matter what we're talking about, he brings in his family. A gratuitous mention. Something connected but not quite relevant to show what great people they are." She rearranged the telephone cord, which in her haste to answer she'd twisted around the lamp. "Like today. It was *Dombey and Son.* Or, rather, Florence Dombey. Her father hates her because she's not a son, girls are shit . . . well, why am I telling you? Anyhow, we'd no sooner finished with the book than he let loose about his own granddaughters. How valued they've always been, such dearly loved girls, just as important as sons, everything perfect in his family. And yesterday there was some excuse to say what a great character Jerry is, and the day before, I forget. No, I remember now, a tribute to Cindy. In the most far-fetched way, he got from Gibbon to Cindy. So what will he do tomorrow?" she said. *"David Copperfield."*

"I don't know about the family, but he's bound to give you that classic scene where Davey bites Mr. Murdstone. Eighteen-forties, those years when parents are sacrosanct, children damn well better stay in line, so how does Dickens manage it? Sort of the way Franklin did, we get a surrogate—Celia, wait and see. A stepfather. One who obliges in every villainous way. He torments the boy, he gives sadistic orders, he sees to it that Mama has no will to interfere. And one evening he puts his hand where Davey's teeth can clamp down on it. In a second the deed is done, one of the great symbolic mutilations and one for which a stepfather can provide the necessary sanction. Hey, Celia, I got carried away."

"Jason, I want to take your course next year. English novel, nineteenth century."

"I'm a hard marker, Miss Sommerville."

"I wonder how you'd mark these Ellsworths." Her tone changed: back to business. "Jason, listen. They're keeping tabs on me. Jerry passed me twice when I went to that school. It's a road that leads no place special, what was he doing there if not—"

"Watching the detective," Jason said.

"And after dinner tonight, Jill found an excuse to get me alone. Not really alone. Out on the porch. I told you about that porch, didn't I? This long line of chairs, and window boxes brimming with pink geraniums that they water twice a day, and off to one side an antique sleigh with more geraniums. Those flashy pink blooms crowded into every inch. Heavenly. So I was standing there for a second, hard to say which is more spectacular, the view out over the railing or inside it, and Jill came up. . . ."

She was silent, reliving the scene. "You're upset about the way Jerry talked to you last night, aren't you?" Jill had said. She had on a yellow sweater and white slacks; the dim lights of the porch shone on the yellow-and-white curves of that amazing figure.

"I can't say I blame you—he really did sound cruel. But he's not cruel, my brother Jerry, he—do you have time to listen?"

Celia nodded and looking inside, into the Ping-Pong

room, where Cindy was huddled in earnest discourse with the two teenage boys.

"Thing is, one of his friends tried it. Suicide, that is. Kid across the street. There was one of those I guess you'd call it an epidemic at the high school. Social pattern is what some psychologist said; suicide gets to be the accepted way for sixteen-year-olds to handle their problems.

"So anyhow, one boy did it, and then another, and then this friend of Jerry's tried. Being fashionable. In the swing of things." The yellow-clad shoulders shuddered. "God. I didn't mean to make a pun. It's just the way they did it was hanging. The first in his own room, and the next—oh, what's the difference? Jerry's friend was in the garage, but he didn't get very far. Maybe he never meant to, it was just one of those gestures that mean: Please look at me. But what happened, his father and mother were devastated. You never saw such frantic people. They went to therapists and parent meetings and encounter groups—I can't remember what all. They'd never had any use for that stuff before, just an ordinary couple who ran a little import-export business, but now they were different people. Especially the mother. She'd always been something of a prude, but now all that therapy talk hitting her at age fifty, she'd say outrageous things. Outrageous for her, that is. All the details of her menopause or how her husband couldn't give her a decent roll in the hay, or gossip about a neighbor, he's getting his on the outside, she would say. That prudish woman. As if everything inside all of a sudden shook loose. And then things really did shake loose, her husband left her; it was all too much."

Easier to look through the window, even though, there in the Ping-Pong room, an argument seemed to be going on. What project did they have in mind, those boys in their Shetland sweaters and plaid shirts, that Cindy was vetoing with that emphatic shake of her head?

"It really got to Jerry. Blew his mind. To see what his friend had done to those parents. A real transformation. Their lives changed. So when that man . . ."

George has turned into "that man." The stiff face with its high forehead, its look of anxious superiority, smoothed out into this bland designation.

"You can see why Jerry turned on you, but the thing to remember, he'd turn on anyone, he really didn't—"

Jill stopped talking. The two boys, with Cindy lagging behind, were coming over. Above the sweaters, their faces were taut with some furtive satisfaction. "Hey, Gillian," the taller one said. "Would you sign this? Give us your autograph?" With a courtesy that was somehow overdone, that had a perceptible smirk in it, he held out a pencil and a piece of paper.

"What is all this?" But Jill knew, she must have had an idea anyhow, otherwise why the suddenly lowered brows, the frown compounded of fear and anger both?

"Hey, it's you, isn't it?" the boy went on. "Page forty. Forty *and* forty-one—neat. Wearing nothing but that little—"

"Bill, shut up," his friend said.

The first boy blinked, but the pleased smirk stayed intact, the hand holding the paper edged closer. "Come on, Gillian. We won't tell anyone. Only other readers. *Connect*—great little magazine, you can trust us."

But as Jill stiffened, took an involuntary step back, it was Cindy that Celia watched. A shifty gleam of something—sly pleasure? lasciviousness?—mixed in with the round ingenuous face, the eye-rolling expression of helplessness, the shrug that said I tried to stop them.

"Gillian. Just sign." Bill's friend, with brusque friendliness. A boy who perhaps was sorry already, wished they had never started.

Jill did sign. She was breathing hard, but she had it under control. One making the best of a bad bargain, even managing a contemptuous little laugh; she took the pencil, bent over, scribbled something on the paper. "Idiot kids," she muttered with an effort as she turned back to Celia.

Celia felt the tension in that effort as she talked to Jason now. You ever hear of a magazine called *Connect*? she started to say, stopped on time, not just because she realized what kind of magazine *Connect* probably was, had to be, but because she had an idea, or at least the glimmer of an idea, of how *Connect* might fit into a larger scheme of things and there was some heavy checking to do first. Okay, save that for another time.

So she simply told Jason that Jill had also introduced the subject of suicide.

"They're really working you over, aren't they?" Jason said.

"You know what? They're making me believe in it. Like a religious conversion. They pound away and pound away, so finally you have to admit, okay, maybe there is something in all that stuff, maybe there is. I still don't think for a minute George killed himself, but they've all been at me. Jill, Marcia, Jerry, their mother. They've made it a possibility. A valid theory. Around here, suicide has credentials. It comes with a plausible background. It's right out of the textbooks. Does that sound wild? Just shows what a snow job they're doing on me."

"Celia, are you thinking of giving up?"

She felt a sudden spurt of anger. There he is, in his protected routine, grading exams, assigning papers, whipping the summer school students into shape—easy for him to talk about giving up. Then she thought, but that's not fair, her one friend, her steady support. Her steady.

She said no, not giving up, in fact tomorrow, at lunch time, her plan is to visit Mattie Haines. Who is Mattie Haines? Les had told her. Used to be maid to the Ellsworths, and since the professor has a strong disinclination to have anyone new take care of him, he keeps her in

Cedar Springs so she can do the cooking for the times when Les goes off and his brother Arnie, who is the standard replacement, takes over.

"Celia, be careful."

"You think I'm going to offend her?"

"You know that's not what I mean. Those people. If they're following you."

"Not exactly following." In her heart, exultation. Maybe this is what she's been wanting, for him also to be conscious of a conspiracy, sense the underlying menace under all that exuberant good will. He even calls them "those people," that denigrating phrase they themselves use against George.

Exultation even though "be careful" is in truth a nonstatement, an expression that leads to nothing. The only sure way to be careful is to give up, back out: a course just repudiated by both of them. Otherwise, careful how? When she comes into the bright kitchen at noon and asks Les where Mattie Haines lives? When, following instructions, she turns left at the laundry and left again at Library Lane, and thence down the hill to the neat row of two-family houses that face the field for the Farmers' Market? Or should she be careful about getting the correct ingratiating note in her voice for the large elderly black woman who answers the bell?

The woman surveyed her. "You selling something? Not interested."

"Mrs. Haines, I'm not selling . . . If I could just talk to you a minute. I mean about Professor Ellsworth."

"You thinking I can help you get a piece of his money? Something for your favorite cause? Think again, Miss, I'm not playing, I won't introduce you, don't even—"

"Look, it's nothing about money. I mean, I work for him, I don't have any—"

"I suppose they told you Mattie Haines was the one to see."

74

"I just want to explain. Oh, please. One minute, can't I come in?"

It was managed somehow, the two of them side by side on the round rag rug. Side by side, but Mattie Haines took up the larger portion; her body in its blue striped dress seemed to reach both sides of the rug at once. But her voice was soft, uncombative, as she said people did it all the time. They couldn't get to him, so they tried through her. Petitioners. Old friends. New friends. Strangers. Price you paid for knowing someone who was filthy rich.

Celia repeated again that far from being interested in money, what she hoped for was any memories Mrs. Haines might have about Roy Ellsworth when he was at school.

"*Miss* Haines." The huge body bent slightly forward.

"Sorry."

"You from the police?"

"Oh, no."

"Or the family?"

Some delicate negotiations needed here? "In fact, I wish you wouldn't tell the family I came."

Mattie Haines snorted. "No fear of that. They don't talk to me, they don't come to see me. Even when they're here for ten days, they don't come to see me; why would I tell them anything?"

Well, an ally: who would have expected it in this house at the bottom of Library Lane? An ally who may or may not do her any good.

The woman was looking at her shrewdly. "So is it to do with that man who maybe killed himself? Roy's old school friend, they said in the paper?"

She admitted that she and George Theroux had both worked at the same university in Boston, and felt herself thereupon subjected to a protracted scrutiny. Possibly she passed because the woman asked would she care for some iced tea.

"That would be nice."

"Maybe you like it with more sugar. Just say the word." Mattie Haines poured from a large green pitcher on the sideboard.

It was fine like this.

"Come sit over here. Some of this candy? Me, last thing I should do is eat it. Take off thirty pounds, the doctor says. Big joke. What size are you? A six?"

"Eight."

"Lucky. Even when I was your age, I never . . . You thirty? All right, thirty-five. Well, even then." Mattie Haines leaned back, glass in one hand, candy in the other, and said she was sorry to disappoint, but if Celia wanted to find out about Roy at school age, any age, she was in the wrong place. "Roy was never my charge. I don't much go for children, if you want the truth. Don't now, didn't then. You don't know where you are. Kids: one day sweet as pie, the next day ready to turn on you. Different with grown ups. I don't care how hard you have to work, just so you can get a routine and stick to it."

So Celia was not going to solve the puzzle of that high-school debacle here. She looked up brightly. "But you did work for them."

"Them? No. I was Miss Suzanne's maid. A full-time job. Keeping her clothes. Taking her phone calls. Opening her packages."

Suzanne: Ellsworth's second wife, the one who had come trailing that remarkable fortune. When Celia looked over she saw Mattie Haines's face was transfused with pleasure, sated, as if the memory of those intimate chores were some sweet making its delectable way down her throat.

"Was she beautiful?"

"She sure was. No, she wasn't. Nose too big. Eyes too close together. Who says you have to be beautiful to get the men?"

"Men. You mean the professor?"

"Him and any other she laid eyes on." The woman put down her glass. "You look surprised. Maybe I shouldn't talk about it."

But she wants to, obviously. Celia murmured that it was long ago; who could be hurt?

"You're so right. She's dead, I bet most of the men are. Not that I ever saw them, she just told me about them."

"She really told you?"

"Why not? She couldn't tell him, her husband, could she? And you have to tell someone or what's the fun?" Mattie Haines pushed the box of chocolates across the table. "I was a good one to tell. I was twenty-five when I went to work for her. Just the age she was. We're like twins, Mattie, she would say. It was part of my job, getting to listen to the stories."

Celia nodded. Twins, but one was having herself a life, the other served as confidante of it. A confidante with the power to sympathize but not judge, listen but not criticize.

"I thought it was thrilling." Mattie Haines walked laboriously across the room to pour more iced tea. "All those men she went to bed with—like the movies. Better than the movies. I was just up from the South, I didn't know, I thought this was how it was for all rich young women. White ones. Their husbands went to work and they had theirselves love affairs. I could tell when she came home in the afternoon. No, that's wrong. She told me when she came home in the afternoon. Called me in and gave me the whole of it. Where they met and which hotel and what she wore and what he looked like. Such a thrill. You slept with some man in the afternoon, and then you sat down for dinner with your own husband." She studied the chocolates, drew back her hand, reached out again. "And nothing to go wrong because all that money, plenty of help in the kitchen to make the dinner and pick up the phone, and a closet full of clothes so if you messed up your best dress playing around, another best hanging in there."

77

Celia finished her drink. The woman is relishing it, loving it. Sitting back in the chair, fleshy arms sagging on the arm rests, folds in her face heavy above the copious chins, she's transported to those days, the favored voyeur, the chosen audience, someone remembering real life.

Well, why be surprised anymore at old people wanting to talk, eager for it? The past is vivid to them, and a listener who will let them recreate it is not a pest but a boon. True about this woman, thrilled to be back in her past as keeper of the wardrobe, and also of Elias Druer, unaware of the discomfort of the hard bench as he looked back with voluptuous pleasure to the titillating horrors of prep school, and as for Professor Ellsworth, what is he doing when he pours into the tape recorder his feelings about David Copperfield and Florence Dombey but transfiguring into acceptable shape some aspect of his own possibly troubled past?

"Don't ask me where she got the men. A married woman, but they always seemed to be on hand. One was this doctor she almost married, but she backed out and chose the professor instead. You'd think he'd hold it against her, but no. And one was a friend of the professor, maybe they taught together. I remember once she was with him in the afternoon, and that night he was coming to dinner. Help me carry it off, Mattie, she said, but she didn't need help, that one." Mattie Haines leaned back, voice tinged with pride, eyes holding a gleam of her own private gratification. "And one of them was black. That's the truth." The big face turned slowly, cast a furtive glance at Celia. "It didn't last. She didn't much like him. She just wanted to see was it different in bed with someone black. Was it different? Now I remind me, she never did tell."

Celia reached out to a blue-and-white bowl on the table. Did they make it at that pottery center the hotel brochure invites them to visit: COME SEE OUR GIFTED ARTISANS AT WORK.

"I once heard there's a name for someone like that. Miss Suzanne. But I don't remember."

"What about the husband?" Then Celia heard what she'd said. The husband: another persona. Not the scholar who delved into an extraordinary memory in order to give eloquent renditions of literature, not the defensive paterfamilias seizing on any excuse to point out the merits of his family. The cuckold, rather, whose wife went to bed in the afternoon with his colleagues.

"Did he object? That what you want to know? Not a peep. Not anyways so anyone could hear. He'd just sit at the table, nice as you please, this nice cool talk with his own wife."

Celia went over to the window. This house was in a hollow; there was not the great expanse of steeples and rooftops and distant mountains that formed one's routine allotment from the porch of the inn. But a picture-postcard quality nonetheless: sprawling bushes and silver birches encircling the gently sloping field where twice a week the farmers might bring their produce. "Maybe he didn't know," she murmured.

"You want to think that, go ahead." The woman heaved herself up from her chair. "A man always knows, don't try to tell me different. He'd have to be blind and deaf, his own wife, carrying on like that."

"What about when she died? Suzanne?"

"You mean the accident? Driving off that cliff? Way I figured it, she was on her way to a date, and she got mixed up, all those different stories she had to make up for her husband, and that's how she lost control. But don't pay that no mind. Maybe she was just going for a ride, and it was raining, the road all skiddy, and poor thing, over she went."

"Were you here with them?"

"It was my time off. They were here alone. Well, not exactly alone. You got all that money, there's always that crowd of servants. But no one close to them. Just the professor and Miss Suzanne and the boy. Roy."

The enigmatic Roy, growing through a chaotic adolescence and what seemed an uneventful adulthood, dying in middle age to leave a family that became their grandfather's obsessive concern. Celia thought about them as she stared at the field. No market today, but the grass was tamped down where on Tuesdays and Saturdays the customers stood, sniffing at boxes of berries, testing the young zucchini for size and freshness.

She murmured something about the family. She wished she knew what they were really like.

"Read the newspaper, you want to know. Two years ago this month. Just read it and find out what some of them are up to."

"The newspaper. Which one? What does it say?"

She spoke too eagerly. Mattie Haines put up a hand, making a fast retreat from an ill-advised position. "I don't tell stories. Just because they don't come to visit me, that don't mean I tell stories." Glowering, burdened with a diffuse anger, she poured herself another glass of iced tea without asking Celia if she wanted one. "They think I'm just a dumb fat woman, but you know what? Right now I have as much money as any of them. Sure, some day they'll be rich, why else would they be hanging around him, but it's today I'm talking about. He pays me a lot. Just for staying on here and filling in when he needs me, a nice big check every month." She had her hand on the back of a chair, which tilted under her shifting weight. "A rich woman," she went on with no inflection. "I go into that bank on Main Street, the one with the pillars, the manager says Good morning, Miss Haines. Seventy-five years old, that's right. A rich old black woman in Cedar Springs, Vermont. Overweight too, did I leave that out?"

What she left out is that she isn't unique. A generation of black women like her, Celia thought. In the only jobs they were trained for, they got respectable wages and passable working conditions and the occasional windfall of second-hand jewelry or clothing, and in return they stayed on. If they had husbands, they ignored them. If there were children, grandmothers brought them up. When there were holidays, they helped the white family enjoy them.

But they have their memories. Memories they can dispense generously, with fluent abandon, recreating a year, an age, a character, a marriage. But memories they can also withhold—that last great exercise of power—so the listener has no way of telling if it's some paltry piece that is missing, or a picturesque one, or the single crucial one without which the past can never be expected to make sense.

8

"JASON, GUESS WHAT? I have it worked out, motive and all. I mean, I know why they killed George. I picked up some information this afternoon and—well, it's all come together." The words were distinct in her mind as she dialed. But no answer. Here she is with this incredible news, and he doesn't answer his phone. While she's been tracking down murderers, has he gone out with one of those graduate groupies, the ones who camp outside the office of the English department's hotshot bachelor? And if he has, why shouldn't he have?

And what's she doing with this kind of thought? To stop it, she turned on the professor's dictation of this afternoon.

"So submission is the order of business for children in the sentimental novel of America in the mid-eighteen-hundreds. Why do we call them sentimental? Well, Celia, see that folder on the second shelf? The one marked SENTIMENTAL NOVEL? Now open it to page two. Does the caption read Young Heroine at Home? Yes, that one. Go on, my dear, you read it."

"'Why Mamma, in the first place I trust every word you say, entirely—I know nothing could be truer; if you were to tell me black is white, Mamma, I should think my eyes had been mistaken. Then everything you tell or advise me to do, I know it is right perfectly. Then I always feel safe when you are near me. . . .'"

"Enough. We get the idea. And you read it perfectly, my dear. The exact combination of the sincerity that won these books their vast audience and the self-abasement that sounds so much like parody. And it's easy, of course, to find these books ludicrous. But the fact is, they touched something deep in the collective heart just because they stemmed from something basic in the prevailing thinking. That little hero- ine whose words you just read may not resemble a real child, but she goes one better; she represents the model real children of that time were supposed to emulate. Accustom your child to immediate acquiescence . . . bring him under perfect subjection . . . instill habits of submission and self- denial: with injunctions like these the authorities laid down the rules for bringing up children. And here in the senti- mental novel was proof that the system worked; that lugu- brious little model is the message."

And what about her message? She switched off the ma- chine. Half past nine. The evening with the graduate groupie will be just starting, no chance that he's come home yet. She went to the phone.

"Jason?"

"Hey, Celia, I just came in. The dean—"

"Jason, listen. I have it worked out, motive and all. I mean, I know why they killed George. It's all come to- gether."

"After just four days, you really—"

She knew how tense she must be from the jolt to her insides. "Would you feel better if it was forty days?"

"Celia, all I said was it seems a very speedy—"

"If things fall into place, should I—"

"Celia, baby, how about just telling me?"

All right, now she knows. She's let herself get too over- wrought. She has to get herself in hand. "It's a long story," she said, and took the final bite of her orange—all she's had, besides a soggy sandwich, since noon.

"Jason, listen. Not one of that family is what Grandpa thinks they are. Not a single one. Where do you want me to start? Jerry—I told you about him. This sallow, sort of shifty character who supposedly was lying on top of a mountain with a trail guide in his hand and three chocolate bars in his stomach at the time George was shot. A stress engineer, the professor told me, and I figured, okay, maybe there are some stress engineers who work from midnight to eight and look like underworld characters." A pause, while she wiped juice from the orange off her skirt. "Well, I was talking to that woman this afternoon. Mattie Haines. And it turned out she had her own reasons for being pissed off at the Ellsworths. There she is, the old family retainer, and they don't come to see her or show her the proper respect—oh, it's the old story. So accidentally on purpose, she let slip that a couple of years ago there was something in the local paper about them. Well, I spent an hour at the newspaper office—their index, my God, must've been done by a five-year-old—and finally I found it. Under *S.,* S for Stolen Cars. Stolen, that is, by Jerry Ellsworth, age twenty-five—well, twenty-five two years ago—from the parking lot behind the movie house and discovered two days later when he happened to sideswipe a car on Route thirty something, and the police—Jason, do you need more details about Grandpa's stress analysis engineer?"

He said he got the picture.

"Well, that got me thinking about the others. Or, rather, about things that had happened with the others. I mean, if Jerry, that exemplary Jerry . . . Anyhow, Marcia and Bernie, take them next. That couple the professor is so pleased with because they stuck together. Not one of those flighty marriages irresponsible young people jump into and then break up at terrible cost to morals and mental growth. Okay. So once I had Jerry spotted as a car thief, I remembered something funny that happened the first night. I was in the lobby after dinner, that bustling place with all the pamphlets about best hotels and maple sugar and come see our exhibit of local crafts. And Marcia and Bernie started talking, suicide, of course, what else does any of them talk to me about, and then a friend of Marcia's came up. Lexa. All bubbly excitement. They just got here and such fun and Greg, that's her husband, would be so tickled because you know how dull these backwater places can be. And in the middle of it all, Bernie disappeared. Just sidled off. One minute deep in this magazine about trout fishing and the next minute gone. A speedy exit up the stairs."

"Lots of reasons why someone wants to get to his room in a hurry," Jason said. "He ate too much of that divine food. He remembered a phone call. He needed a sweater."

"But what was funny was them. Lexa and Greg. I mean, Lexa didn't greet him. He was standing a foot away and she ignored him."

"Maybe she didn't see him."

"You can't not see Bernie. He has this round mushy face. Besides, he wears peculiar clothes. Peculiar, I mean, for up here. Everyone else all tweedy and Shetland sweaters, and there he is in a dark blue business suit. The kind you really wear for business. Anyhow, Lexa ignored him, he ignored her. As if he wasn't there. And then he was not there and it didn't seem to make a difference. Not for her or for Greg either."

"Maybe there was an old feud."

"Couldn't be. She kept saying, the four of us, we'll do this, we'll do that. Like some great restaurant for lunch tomorrow and some sensational find in an antique store."

"So if they had lunch . . ."

"But they didn't. Marcia said they had to spend all day with Grandpa. Which is an obvious lie because Grandpa very carefully doles out oh, maybe, half an hour at a time to visiting relatives."

"Celia, is what you're saying . . . do you think Bernie isn't her real husband?"

Glory be! From where he's sitting it may indeed look as if all this has been very speedy—superficial?—but in the end he's in there with her. Without any need for extra words or spelled out facts, the ideas transmitted, held up to a joint consensus. But he did add that it was just a speculation, they couldn't be—

"Positive. I know. So I called their house. I mean, Marcia's house."

"How'd you know her name?"

"Good question. This Lexa had mentioned an antique store. The Golden Horn on Long Island. Well, a cinch to get that number, and I told the man I'd been with my friend Lexa looking for antique mirrors, maybe he remembered us—and quick as a bunny, proving how he had his eye on the ball, he chimed in with Mrs. Sturdevant. Blessed man. Honestly, Jason, it wasn't till I got off the phone that I thought, suppose her name had been something ordinary like Smith or Brown, pages and pages in the phone book."

"Celia, go on."

"Well, only six Sturdevants listed by information. The first didn't answer, and the second was obviously wrong, a sulky child who said Mommy was in the kitchen would I wait, and the third I forget, and the fourth was this very practiced maid. Mrs. Sturdevant? Sorry, Mrs. S was in Vermont for ten days; did I want to leave a message for Mr. S? So I said I was an old college friend and I hadn't seen Mrs. Sturdevant for a long time, not since she'd been married to her former husband. And that maid—not so practiced, now I think of it, a really trained maid would not have spilled the beans so readily to a stranger—anyhow, the woman said with a little giggle, did I mean when she'd been Mrs. Hays. Now, Jason, it just happens that Bernie's name is Lenox." She found a crumb of the sandwich and ate it. "So—"

"So far from being married to the man her grandfather

thinks she is, would like her to be, she's in fact on husband number three."

"At least three. Who knows, maybe a Mr. X in there too."

Good going, the voice at the other end told her.

"Next Gillian. Jill. Did I tell you about her? This sensational looking . . . really, it's her figure that's sensational. Anyhow, she was talking to me last night, suicide again, like I told you, part of the conversion of Celia Sommerville—we were talking and these two boys sashayed over. Much leering and ogling, I thought it was big bouncy Jill in her voluptuous sweater and white pants. But then they asked for her autograph because they'd seen her on pages forty and forty-one of *Connect*—What'd you say?"

"Nothing."

"So you do know it?"

"Can't help seeing it on the newsstands," he said discreetly.

"So at the time I didn't think anything of it. But after hearing about Jerry. Anyhow, I stopped in at this stationery store, let's hope they never find out who I am, and *Connect* was there, all right. Not featured in the window, we're a respectable town, after all, but in a display case in back—Jason, you should see her. No, on second thought, maybe you shouldn't see her."

"Your Jill?"

"Everyone's Jill, once those pictures get around. A different name, but no question. The hair, the eyes, the mouth, the . . . Well. Grandpa's serious girl, the merchandise expert, decked out in stockings and a garter belt."

"Different kind of merchandising," he murmured.

"Somewhat."

"Celia, incidentally, where'd you get time for all this? Phoning, research, more phoning, shopping."

"I skipped dinner. No, not exactly. I brought home an orange and a sandwich." She checked the wax paper from the sandwich, but as she knew, nothing left. "That suspicious family, they're probably chewing their nails this minute. Where is she, what's she up to, why didn't she come down?"

"That suspicious family, of whom three, as you say, are—"

"Four," she said.

"What's that?"

"The youngest Cindy, she's also in the club. A sulky high-school student whose grandfather has her set up to be a math whiz."

"Can't a high-school kid be sulky and also know her math?"

"Look. I don't even blame her. This dignified inn, all these guests in their sensible clothes and their books on birds and their visits to the local crafts barn—it must drive her up a wall. Even worse, her two boyfriends left this morning, well, they have Jill's autograph, at least they have that. Oh, Jason, sure I feel for that fresh Cindy, feel for all of them, kept in line by a grandfather's stubborn whims. But once you start suspecting . . ."

"Did you give her some tricky math questions to fake her out?"

"Even better. She wears this sweatshirt. S.H.S., white on green. Well, I have a friend who teaches in New York—Louise—and I asked her what those initials might signify, and of course she knew. Sheridan. One of those schools that cater to kids who have trouble making it at more rigorous places. Their parents pay a mint so they can stand around looking dissolute and be spoon-fed the basic stuff and drilled in the technique of taking the SATs. You know. Anyhow, I was lucky there too. A janitor or someone was around, and he gave me the name of the headmistress, and she told me—"

"Just like that, out of the blue, a headmistress would come clean about a pupil?"

She heard the note of puzzlement—disapproving puzzlement?—and gripped the receiver harder. "I made up a name and said I had a couple of children and Cindy had applied for a baby-sitting job in August."

"You really went all out, didn't you?"

Such studied neutrality in his voice. Does it mean he's in favor of her having gone all out? He thinks she overstepped some line of delicacy and good taste? He'd feel better if luck and ingenuity hadn't let her accomplish this in so short a time?

"Jason, they're a conspiracy. All four of them in cahoots. Five if you count the mother. You have to count the mother; she's in charge, she masterminds it all. I mean, if you were here, if you could size them up. Anyhow, Cindy. She's been suspended. She cheated on an exam. A math exam, no less, to keep from failing. The woman obviously didn't want to be explicit, she went in for lots of innuendos, but she managed to make clear that no one in her right mind would hire Cindy Ellsworth for the care of impressionable children."

"So they're conning Grandpa, is that what you think?"

She was suddenly exhausted. All this talking, added to the hours on the phone already. She said it was certainly what the record seemed to show.

"And is it your further idea—Celia, I don't mean to sound like a district attorney—do you suppose George found that out, or rather knew it from all the cozy old-boy phone calls with Roy, and he threatened to tell the professor unless they paid up, and since their inheritance, after all, was at stake—"

"So they killed him. Yes." She added with a deep sigh that it all fit in.

"Not quite all. It doesn't answer the question of why Roy as an adolescent went in for those bouts of paranoid anger—it's what you told me—against his father."

Imagine: an objection. She's turned the whole damaging

and inexplicable circumstance of George's death into something simple, obvious, reasonable, neat, and here is Jason with an objection.

"Jason, we're talking about a fifteen-year-old, everyone knows that they. . . I mean, adolescent pressures, ego identity, like that Mr. Druer said. Besides, maybe he was exaggerating, an old man, inevitable that he'd build up his own role, make the boy sound even more disturbed. . . . Okay. You're right. Not everything is explained. Not quite everything. But it's what that policeman said he needed. A motive."

"It's that, all right," he said after a pause.

Her hand on the phone was damp. "Jason, I know what you're thinking. I was prejudiced before I even came up here. You even said it. You can't convict people long distance. Well, I did convict them, it's true. Long before I saw them I figured them as guilty. It's what I started the second I came. Suspecting them. Disliking them. Looking for a motive for their guilt. But now that the motive has turned up, should I just ignore it? I mean, because I was so wrongheaded and prejudiced before, should I not go to the police with my findings now?"

This time no pause; his voice came promptly. Of course she has to tell the police. It's not even open to question. If he sounded skeptical a minute ago, it's only because of the speed of this whole business. Four days. Four amazing days. And the fact is, she's done a spectacular job. That whole conspiracy, as she rightly calls it, nailed down. In just a few ingenious strokes, to uncover the duplicity that five people have spent years putting together. Celia, go to it.

9

"WE MOVE ON THIS morning, Celia, my dear. I'm going to try to remember a few lines from George Eliot's *Mill on the Floss*. If you bear with me a second. . . . Yes. I think I have it. 'They trotted along and sat down together. . . . And the mill with its booming; the great chestnut tree under which they played at houses; their own little river, the Ripple, where the banks seemed like home, and Tom was always seeing the water rats while Maggie gathered the purple plumy tops of the reeds . . .' Of course there may be a word or two wrong, and you'll check it, my dear, as usual. But you get the point. It is eighteen sixty, and fictional children have got moving. They no longer stand around waiting for life to deal the next blow. They're not even wan and frail. In fact, they work hard at the serious business of childhood, which as anyone knows is to get in on all the benefits the entertainment world of nature has for grabs. To this end, they trot along, preferably to some place out of calling distance from home. They fish. They swim. They fight. They consider an hour well spent watching a bug or a leaf or the foam on the water. And they stay away rather longer and get a lot more disheveled than those in charge find desirable. In short, far from being idealized principles of goodness, they begin to look like children—Celia, can't you see them?"

Well, of course she can see them. His eloquence can bring anything to life. There they are, a boy and girl who are testament to the changing times, running, fishing, looking rosy. What she can't see is him. What will happen to this man when his illusions are shattered? When the stable marriage, the child's articles on mathematics, the career in merchandising—when they all go up in smoke. A possible heart attack, they had said, in case he heard of the death of Roy's old school friend, someone he barely knew, hadn't thought of for forty years. So suppose he hears the truth about Roy's children; a man so fixed on the subject of children he's writing a book about them.

"But of course this is not the whole story. The young Maggie pays for that bright, volatile, independent spirit. What we today find dashing and admirable, her own generation found wanton and wildly irresponsible. Because the fact is, for all the new indulgences, the culture of eighteen-sixty still views the child as a small machine for obedience. Renunciation is the obligatory mode, as docility remains the admired look—well, Celia, we'll develop this further this afternoon."

Ah. But considering what she's now going to do, will there be an afternoon session? Can one count on Life After Disclosure? It's true, she told herself on the way to the police station, that it's not on her. It is Officer Hurley, not Celia Sommerville, who will quietly ask those people to accompany him, monitor their phone calls, remind them of their rights: Hurley, the agent of punishment.

Still, when she stood in front of the red brick building that also held Victory Sporting Goods and the Water Department and Sanitation, the tremors hadn't stopped. Not open to question, Jason had said in his voice of quiet reasonableness, but at this instant the questions seem enormous. Must she do it right this minute? Isn't there some reason to put it off? The ruin of the Ellsworth family—could there be some other way?

Well, maybe Hurley won't be here. Maybe he's at that wholesome lunch prepared by his wife for him and the two small boys. Then she can come back down, try on the heavy white sweater in the window of Victory's that she doesn't remotely need but that in a spasm of heady gratefulness for having been let off the hook she will buy.

He was there. Officer Hurley? Go right in. Even a little complacence in the nod of the policeman at the desk, as if to say, We knew you'd be back.

But if Hurley had made such assumptions, they didn't show through his careful courtesy. How is she enjoying her stay in Cedar Springs? Is she finding the work with Professor Ellsworth interesting? Has she had a chance to take in the local sights? Small-town hospitality dispensed for a couple of irrelevant minutes before he leaned forward and by his alert posture and keen look signified that it was time to get down to business.

Her business was what he had asked for on her first visit. A motive. A motive to make it plausible that the Ellsworth family would want to kill George. And now, she said, she has one. The most convincing motive of all, which is to save the inheritance they are presumably in line to get from Professor Ellsworth. But first she has to talk to him a little about this concerned man. His great pride in his family. His delight in their successes. His gratuitous mention, on any occasion, of what exemplary people they are.

"Except they're not so exemplary at all. I found out by accident. I heard about Jerry Ellsworth, that stolen car business . . . well, that's old hat to you, I guess, and lord knows how you hushed it up so his grandfather didn't hear. But what it did for me, it put a lot of things that had happened in different perspective. Everything shifted . . ." She told it in pedestrian detail. Marcia and Bernie. Jill. Cindy. Plus that eagle-eyed mother. Every twist and turn of her own exploration. She talked steadily, through the ringing of his phone and the appearance at the door of two policemen and some speedy driving and horn blowing down in the parking lot that indicated there might be more police activity in Cedar Springs after all than the fetching of cats down from trees, and when it was over, he whistled.

"Some very snappy detective work there, Miss Sommerville."

"Thanks."

"We could use someone like you on our staff."

She received the words with sedate modesty.

"I don't think there's a detail you missed."

Still another compliment, imagine, from the inflexible Officer Hurley.

He looked out at the parking lot too. Quiet down there now—only a boy pushing a shopping cart loaded with bags of cat food. Then he said what a shame she'd had to go through all that effort for nothing.

"I don't understand."

Hurley put down his pencil. "Things aren't always as clear-cut as they seem, Miss Sommerville. Especially when you're dealing with a character like Professor Ellsworth. A very complicated man, that one."

What is this! "Oh, I'm sure."

"I've known him a long time. Our whole force watches out for him. He's our charge, you might say."

The local millionaire: I bet.

"Every month or so, I drop in. Check on him, check on the house." Hurley gave a hard look at his desk pad, as if the latest report were written there. Cellar window of Ellsworth house cracked. Back door needs realignment. "Miss Sommerville, you're helping him write a book, you're connected with his literary work, am I right? So you see one side of him. But here in Cedar Springs, I see another side."

She said it must be, hmm, interesting.

"We have long conversations. Not just about locks and windows. I tell him about my family, he tells me about his," the drawling voice said. "Sometimes life brings disappointments. Nothing goes exactly the way you planned it. Not for you and me, Miss Sommerville, not even for a man like Professor Ellsworth." He leaned back in his chair: Officer Hurley, back-porch philosopher. "What you discover is that despite any expectations you may have for your own family they're going to lead their own lives."

She opened her mouth but said nothing.

"Sometimes you make the discovery sooner, sometimes later," his textbook voice said. "But in the course of events you inevitably do discover it."

"Listen. Are you trying to tell me Professor Ellsworth knew something about what his grandchildren really did?"

"Not something. Closer to everything. It started with the Jerry business. Hushed up, did you say? Only insofar as Ellsworth money was used to pay off the injured party and fix his car and convince the newspapers that any further articles would be a mistake. And, of course, keep Jerry out of jail. For someone with Jerry's record, not so easy to keep him out of jail." Hurley's voice had lost its speculative note; it was fitting for one who had shifted from philosophy to facts. "Wouldn't be surprised if after that the professor went the same route you did," he added. "You know how it goes. You think back to something that maybe rubbed you the wrong way, look at it upside down."

"My God."

"Don't let it upset you, Miss Sommerville. He wasn't upset. I remember what he said. 'If they're your family, you accept them': his exact words. 'However they turn out'— it's what he told me—'best to remember you have a part in it.'"

"What does that mean?"

Hurley shrugged: just reporting facts, Ma'am, just reporting facts.

"But the way he talks about them . . ." She let herself

replay the words: fine young man . . . house afire . . . math whiz.

"He's very proud," Hurley explained: back to speculation. "He wants his reputation the way he wants it. He's in there working at it."

What a mistake she's made. That's the real pride, of course. Not to exult in one's family as shining people, but to invent the shine, concoct for public consumption a fictitious story about it.

Does Hurley know what she's thinking? "Look at the life he leads," he said. "In that room of his twenty-four hours a day. He could easily go out. Take rides. Pay visits. Or just sit on his own lawn, under his own trees. A man with his money, he could even travel. But that would mean someone would see him in a wheelchair. Or being carried. He'd be exposed as a helpless invalid. This way he's just an old man who happens to keep a plaid blanket over his legs."

She felt cold. Chilled and dizzy at once. Her ingenuity, her clever guesses, her sly tactics. "But if you knew all this, why'd you let me—" She stopped. She knows why he sat with glum patience while she went through that long saga about her exploits. Because it gives him sanction to say things like, Things aren't as clear-cut as they seem, Miss Sommerville. Or, Life brings disappointments. Or, Nothing goes exactly the way you want it. He can be sage, powerful, tolerant, omniscient—the small-town police officer in a position to assert himself.

Then she thought of something. "Maybe, like you say, Professor Ellsworth knows the truth about his family. But that doesn't mean they know that he does. I mean, they could still think they had to—"

"Oh, they know, all right. Leave it to his daughter-in-law. Mrs. Roy Ellsworth. A smart woman, that one. What she doesn't know you could put into an acorn." He allowed himself a quick smile. "Fact, she once said it to me. We kid each other, me and my father-in-law. A good system. Keeps everything on an even keel."

"But if everyone has this great understanding about everyone else"—she heard the petulant note of disappointment in her voice—"I mean, if it's all out in the open, why that elaborate charade with Bernie?"

"Appearances, appearances," Hurley said with his studied sageness. "They know how important it is to him. Besides, that Bernie business, that was the first show they put on, long before other things got out, as you say, in the open—a lot of dirty linen would have to be publicly washed if they tried to change it now."

An answer for everything. She knew she should push back her chair, stand up, think up some remark that would allow her to walk out with a measure of jauntiness, but for a moment she felt unable to move.

Hurley was watching her. "I know your concern, Miss Sommerville. Believe me, I appreciate the position. But leave it alone. Best advice I can give." If he didn't reach across the desk to give a patronizing pat to her hand, his voice insinuated that he might have. "You go on doing what you're here for—helping the professor write his book—and leave it to us to find out if there's anything amiss about George Theroux's death."

10

A SENSE OF FAILURE, how it changes everything. The whole aspect of the world distorted, turned sour. That pretty picturesque street down which you were walking half an hour ago, what a vulgar display of gimcrack items in the store windows. The old man whose smile warmed you with its sweetness as you went up the steps, he's nothing but a simpering old sot. Even the gazebo, that intricately carved and freshly painted treasure in the middle of a green, simply a conceit, a cutesy toy that grown men suppose can embody the spirit of their town. As for those distant mountains, what purpose do they have except to loom darkly, remind people of their new demeaning status?

And if the world from now on will look worse, what about her? She walked past Jefferson's and thought, that patronizing pat that Hurley just refrained from giving her, that must be her lot from now on. From whom? Well, first of all, from Jason. How else can he react when she tells him? He won't say, Celia, you went too fast, you had all the answers before you started looking, but he will think it. In fact, he has been thinking it. Well, he's right. From the moment she saw them in the dining room, they were not individuals entitled to their quirks, their good looks, their boisterous fun. Right away she thought, ha, conspiracy, that word that connotes sneakiness, unpleasantness, menace, stealth. No, even before she saw them in the dining room, when she sat with Jason in that dowdy restaurant and in the back of her mind was the confident theory that they had killed George. Sight unseen, she had drawn the outlines of a portentous cloud labeled ENEMY and slipped them into it.

And what was their fault, when you came down to it? They wanted to get their hands on the family fortune. To this end, they would toady to an old man, put up with his whims, vacation at a place that bored them, disrupt their schedules, connive, flatter, lie . . . in short, do what the younger generation the world over does in order to inherit the money of an older one.

Celia held on to this thought, this tolerant rationalization—they were not so bad, they were not so bad—all through the afternoon session with Professor Ellsworth and the walk back to the Inn and the nap she tried to take in her sun-drenched room. She even focused on it when she went down to the lobby and joined the patient crowd—the woman hiker, the couple with their bird books, a local family out on the town, a tall thin man with a diffident smile she had not seen before—all of them waiting for the curtained doors of the dining room to open.

But when she saw the effusive group at the table where the professor's misguided good will had placed her, she had to face the truth. She still does not like them. It's probably a commentary on her—her stubbornness, intransigence, small mindedness, bigotry—but she really doesn't like them, doesn't trust them, wishes to God she knew some way to get something on them.

Deciding what to order, they were at their most effusive. Roast beef? No use asking for it rare, the chef obviously hasn't the ability to oblige. Chicken? Jesus, not again. Lamb? Dependable, but it's probably left over from last night. Fish? Fish up here can be divine, but it can also be something out of the freezer and a waste of breath asking Emmy Lou because she always says fresh. As for Jerry, what's he doing getting in on the act, he had a hamburger not half an hour ago at the crummy place in town; oh, he can quit shaking his head, Cindy saw him, she definitely did.

And they didn't talk about suicide. For the first time since she was with them, that topic did not form the mainstay of their conversation. Maybe, she thought, they feel they have made the point. Or maybe one of that eagle-eyed bunch saw her walking in at noon to the police station and surmised what had happened and realized that from now on they were home free. Or best of all, Hurley told them. That loyal friend of the family passed the word that the heat is off, no more need to put on a show for Celia Sommerville; yes, the whole thing is certainly a big laugh.

That nuisance out of the way, they could subside into complacent griping. Wouldn't you think in a town like this it would be possible to find a decent black cardigan? (Marcia and Jill). He said let him fix the carburetor but anyone can tell that guy doesn't know shit about carburetors (Jerry). You absolutely would not believe the magazines they have out there in the lobby (Cindy). She said three spades when she meant three clubs, that's how far gone she is (Madeleine Ellsworth).

Jill was talking—the lethargic salesgirl and the inadequate selection and the price, you'd have to be insane to pay it—when Celia heard a voice above them. "Aren't you the Ellsworth family?" She looked up: the tall thin man she'd been standing next to before the dining room opened. He repeated it—"Excuse me, but is this the Ellsworth family?"—and she realized he had a lilting voice along with a diffident smile. The lilt, however, had to be repeated still another time before the incurious faces turned to him. He wanted to talk to them, he said. When he added that his name was Lee Elliott, Madeleine motioned Cindy to move over and told Jerry to fit a chair into the empty space.

"Good. So you know the name."

"Roy used to say something about a cousin."

"Second cousin." Again that small apologetic note; it went with the thinning gray hair, soft cheeks, bony frame—a man who was not so much thin as wispy. "Strictly speaking, not even second cousin," he amended, as those at the table responded with little murmurs of amazement. "We pretended to be cousins; when you're six or seven years old, a cousin is just about the best thing you can have. God's gift to boyhood. Someone to be chums with, but you don't have to feel all competitive, like with a brother. Besides, when the visit is over, you go your different ways."

"Cousins but not cousins." Jerry sounded surly. "What is this!"

Mr. Elliott pulled his chair closer; in his lilting voice he explained it. His mother and Professor Ellsworth's second wife Suzanne were cousins. That is, his maternal grandmother and Suzanne's mother—if he's going too fast they should stop him—the two of them were sisters. So when the real cousins used to see each other, only natural for them to bring along their children, who were him and Roy, who happened to be exactly the same age.

"Of course this all happened a long time ago. To this young lady"—a benign nod at Cindy—"it must seem like ancient history. But for me, those visits could be yesterday. Roy and I, what a pair. Anyone who saw us, we said we were cousins; it established a bond. You folks, a big family, you have each other, maybe you don't see the need. Or maybe you do," he allowed, giving each of them a shy look in turn. Even Bernie—does he regard Bernie, in his dark suit and red tie as one of Roy's offsprings? "Anyhow, for all our pretending, we always knew the truth. About the relationship, I mean. Children make a big deal about particulars like that. Roots, who's related to whom—all part of what's important."

"A cousin for my father." Jill's sweater tonight was red and black.

"Not a real cousin, dopey," Cindy said.

"Anyhow, it's neat."

"It was neat." Mr. Elliott brushed away the crumbs at his place. "Except when we were ten years old, it all ended. The fun times, I mean. That was when Suzanne lost her life in some terrible car crash. My poor mother, she cried and cried. Her beautiful Suzanne. I cried too, even though I couldn't believe it. That Roy and I, we wouldn't be playing together any more."

"Wouldn't his father let you?"

"Oh, let," he said sadly. "He was a nice man, I guess. The best. But it wasn't him my mother was related to."

"So you never saw my father again?" Marcia asked.

"Oh, you know how things are. One way or other, we kept in touch." Unexpectedly, he blushed—Celia saw the stain rise on the hollow cheeks, past the gray eyebrows, up to the thinning strands of hair. That busy Roy, she thought. Phone calls year after year to his old school friend George, now in touch, whatever that means, with this wispy non-cousin.

He was sorry, Lee Elliott added, to hear about Roy's death.

An appropriate silence followed this; after it, Madeleine introduced each of the family in turn and then asked Lee Elliott what he was doing here in Cedar Springs.

"I'm not sure. Maybe you can help me." Diffidence, once more.

"Come again?" Jerry looked up from his uneaten dinner.

"I read about that man who committed suicide right here at the inn. That is, they think maybe he committed suicide. But maybe not. A Mr. Theroux. George Theroux."

For once, Celia was on track with the Ellsworth family: an involuntary participant of the communal jolt that went around the table, causing eyes to widen, backs to stiffen, throats to utter murmurous little gasps.

102

"Why should news about George Theroux interest you?" Trust Madeleine Ellsworth to retain composure.

"He came to see me three weeks ago. No, two and a half. A Saturday afternoon. Not me, really, my factory in Nashua, New Hampshire. Elliott Enterprises. Well, you wouldn't exactly call it a factory. A workshop, rather. Me and a couple of assistants. We build tables. Modern, from my own design. Wood laminated with Formica." A smile accompanied every apologetic qualification. "Modern but elegant," he said.

"Tables," Celia said, and closed her lips, conscious that they had opened on one word too many.

"He was interested in buying one. He spent almost two hours looking us over. I can't say it's a big operation, even though a store in Providence handles us and one in Stanford and I'm talking right now to this very interested place out on Long Island."

You must be mistaken. George would never want a modern table. I know what kind of table he wanted. Mahogany, with two leaves, eighteen inches each, and authentic period decoration. To go with his Chippendale chairs and mahogany sideboard. He would never have gone to a small workshop. He would never have gone to Nashua, New Hampshire. It was someone else by the same name. George Theroux, not so unusual. . . . Celia didn't say this or anything else.

"He said he'd think about it and let me know. He didn't let me know. That's not out of the ordinary," the lilting voice said. "If everyone who seemed to be interested gave you an order . . ."

"What did he look like?" Marcia asked.

"Tall. Broad. Let's see." Don't say pompous, Celia thought. "Stiff. No, that's not it either. More, mmm, exacting. He asked me question after question. He wanted to be sure of getting things right."

"Sounds like that man," Jill said.

George, did you know if you came up here and acted in all these odd and incomprehensible ways you would be reduced to "that man"?

"It's not such a usual name. Not really unusual, but not usual. So when someone came into the shop and left a Vermont newspaper."

Emmy Lou, starting to clear the table, reached for Jerry's full plate, pulled back, then remembered and reached out again.

"A Vermont paper with the story. And I thought, funny thing. Man talks to me about one of my tables, and two weeks later there he is, shot in the chest in Cedar Springs," he went on in his singsong way. "The town where my mother used to take me to visit Roy. Even the Inn. Sometimes Suzanne had us all here for lunch. Do you know how old this building is?" This again to Cindy, possibly the most unappreciative repository of such information. "Seventeen ninety-six. No, make it ninety eight. Fact. They've added wings, of course, fixed up things like plumbing, but the porch, the roof, this room, it all was here. Just imagine. So when I read about it. The Cedar Springs Inn. It just nagged at me, the oddness of it, and finally this afternoon . . ." His slender hands went out: Here I am, folks. "And I looked in the register, and there's your name. Ellsworth. Another coincidence."

Now? Yes, now—Celia saw Madeleine draw herself up. "Not such a coincidence at all." The large features leaned forward. "That man came to visit his old prep school. The school is one he and my husband went to. We're here because this is where my father-in-law has chosen to live and this week is his birthday."

It took Lee Elliott a minute to absorb this, these hard facts strung out on the chain of Mrs. Ellsworth's metallic voice. Then there was a lilting sigh. "Think of that. We could have chatted about Roy, Mr. Theroux and I. Instead of all that talk about veneers and wood and dovetail joints, we could have exchanged reminiscences. Roy at six. Roy at sixteen." Then the wispy face brightened. "You know what? You say the professor lives here? I'm the only member of my family left, Suzanne's last remaining relative. I'm sure he'd like to see me."

Mrs. Ellsworth spoke quickly. This would not be advisable. Not advisable at all. The professor was very weak. Visitors were strictly limited to five minutes. No one but the immediate family was allowed.

"That so. Pity. Oh, no dessert, thanks. Well, yes, I would like coffee." Because Emmy Lou was at hand waiting for dessert orders.

Another session of speculation: doing research for everyone, Cindy walked over to the cake wagon across the room. Then Bernie said, "Leroy!"

"Now what?" Marcia regarded him with her usual composed annoyance.

Bernie had his notebook open; above the white shirt and red tie, the round face was beaming. "I was just jotting the name in my notebook. Lee Elliott. Lee. And then I thought, Roy, and I realized. If you put them together, it's a name. Leroy." He pronounced it with a triumphant stress on the first syllable.

"You know, that's right." Mr. Elliott looked pleased too. "Now I think of it, someone did make the connection once. We took it as a sign, Roy and I. It meant in some special way we were meant to be together. Leroy," Lee Elliott repeated with dreamy pleasure. "Now where were we when it happened? Up here? Colorado? No, it was that place they had in Florida. My mother and I always visited Suzanne. Don't ask me why. Well, do ask me," he said, and sent his qualifying smile around the table. "We were the poor branch of the family. Oh, not really poor, don't think that. Just poor like anyone would be in relation to the kind of money Suzanne had. So that's the way things go. The rich

105

ones do the inviting, the poor branch comes running." He smiled his thanks at Emmy Lou, who set down his coffee. "So there we were, and someone came in and sang out the name. Leroy! Two crazy kids, we started giggling. God, it's so long ago. But Roy never forgot. That generous man, whatever we had together, he never let it be lost. That I know, because." He stopped. A complete stop. For once, no diffident correction to amend the didactic remark. Just the same flustered, blushing, semi-embarrassed halt she had noted before.

If anyone else noted it, they didn't question it. They were busy sorting out desserts. Jill, you get the pie? Cindy, this mess with whipped cream, this for you? Bernie, did you want melon? Lee Elliott waited and then cleared his throat. He was sorry none of them could help him. He had just got this bee in his bonnet. He'd driven over in the express hope. But he'd head home now. A three-hour drive over second-class roads, he wanted to make it before twelve. And it was nice meeting all of them, but he could see: some things just have to be a mystery forever.

The hell they do. Celia felt the fervor rising within her. By the time Lee Elliott had stood, her chair was already pushed back. Fast, but not fast enough. "I'll just walk you to your car," Madeleine Ellsworth said, and with the deftest of proprietary motions put her hand on his arm. At which point how could anyone intervene without going in for the kind of argument that reason had so far dictated as being inexpedient and counterproductive?

11

"SHE DIDN'T WANT me to talk to him, that was obvious," Celia said to Jason on the phone. "That masterful grip on his arm, the speedy exit—she was keeping him from me. Making sure I couldn't get at him. And I could have said, Oh, excuse me, I'd like to talk to Mr. Elliott. I could have, but I really couldn't. Without exposing every nasty and mistrustful thought in my head, I couldn't."

An understanding assent from the other end. She loosened her grip on the phone. Telling him about the debacle at the police station had been less painful than she'd expected. He received her story with the stunned dismay that implied it had been his debacle too. He also had been counting on that solution; he'd let himself hope. If any complacence colored his thoughts, any hint that he'd known in advance it wouldn't work, he was too nice or too tactful to let it show.

"That Madeleine Ellsworth—she plays everything right. I mean, from the beginning, she had it programmed. Each of them getting at me about suicide. But each of them mentioning a different aspect of it, having a different pitch—that was no accident. She scheduled it. She assigned the parts. Maybe she even rehearsed them in advance—Jason, do you believe it?"

He believes it.

"Except she didn't know that Lee Elliott would show up. That set her back. Especially when he said he was going to visit Professor Ellsworth. She tipped her mitt on that one. I mean, she went too far. Five minute visits! Only the family allowed! No way she was going to let Lee Elliott get together with the professor, that's for sure.

"But she's not going to keep me from seeing him. Elliott, I mean. A man George visited, spent hours with, on a fake pretext."

"Celia, you sure it was fake?"

"You mean, George might have wanted a table laminated with Formica? Oh, Jason, you don't know George. So why did he go? Why?" She leaned back in the chintz-covered armchair. "There was a Saturday, now I remember, when he said he couldn't see me. Something about grading papers, I thought that was funny; he wouldn't be giving his big exam for another week." A defensive little laugh. "Not that we kept track of each other every minute over weekends." She paused. Actually, they had kept track of each other every minute over weekends. An engagement—that interval like nothing before or after. Solicitude, possessiveness, tender accommodation, lust. Anyhow, she added, she is going there. To Nashua. She's already studied the maps. A cross-lots drive, so to speak, the roads won't be so hot, nothing like the north-south highways. But Elliott made it, after all. And if she leaves first thing in the morning.

"Celia, what about—"

"Professor Ellsworth? I know. I feel terrible. I called Lester to say I was sick. Thank the lord for Lester; I couldn't lie to the professor."

A short silence while they both are thinking the same thing. The professor who lies to himself—Hurley has said it. Such valiant feats of bragging and self-delusion. Such hard ferocious pride. Such sadness.

"Jason, all those stories he keeps telling. The estimable

Jerry. That smart little trick Cindy. His wonderful Jill. Marcia."

"Don't think about it. It doesn't bear thinking about. Celia, call the instant you get back—when will that be?"

"Elliott said three hours—I should be there by noon. From there on, you can figure."

Actually, it was eleven-thirty when she stopped on the main street of Nashua and got directions, and a few minutes later when she drove up to the small low building on a quiet street at the edge of town and asked the man in overalls at the door whether Lee Elliott was there.

He was there and he asked her to come in, but plainly he had trouble recognizing her. For a second she felt hurt: had she been so inconspicuous among all those large, high-colored, good-looking women? Then she realized: sitting at their table, she worked at inconspicuousness, at not talking.

Well, she's talking now. She told it quickly, neatly. She had been engaged to George Theroux, and because his visit here—a look around the cluttered workshop—because it seemed to her so odd, so bristling with anomalies, she wants to know more about it.

Lee Elliott put out his hands. "What can I tell you? He was very interested. He wanted all the details. How the table converts in one operation to half its size—well, look, there's one closed up over there—by this simple pivoting mechanism, and the overlapping frames that make the legs, and the way the plywood top is veneered with ash on one side and laminated on the other with Formica."

His long, wispy face was anxious, expectant, and she produced the obligatory admiration. The table is beautiful. Yes, yes, she can see. The way the legs visually repeat the folding planes of the top—terrific. But she still wonders. What was George doing here?

At the other end of the room, the man in overalls turned on a machine that made a rattling noise and sent out clouds of dust, but Lee Elliott asked him to hold it. "Our tables aren't cheap. Not cheap at all. And that Mr. Theroux, such a careful, deliberate man. I figured, well, before he puts down several thousand dollars . . ."

"How did he hear about you?"

"I didn't exactly ask. One of those magazines that tells about avant-garde furniture had a story about us, I thought—"

"Mr. Elliott, I have to tell you. George didn't read magazines that pictured avant-garde furniture. And he would never have put down a nickel. Not for that table. The table he wanted was an antique mahogany one, or a model that exactly reproduced antique. Something to go with the set of eight Chippendale chairs with cut velvet upholstery that he inherited from his family. Honestly, Mr. Elliott, can you imagine someone with eight Chippendale chairs buying that table over there?"

"I don't understand." Diffidence had turned to dismay; she'd hurt his feelings.

"Look. Your table is a dream. If I had the money I'd buy one in a flash. All I'm saying, George Theroux didn't come here to buy one. He came for some other reason. I'm trying to find out what it was."

"I gave him a tour." The lilting voice was hesitant, troubled. "I explained to him about workmanship. I showed him some of the machines."

She thought quickly. "Do you think . . . well, if you wouldn't mind giving me the same sort of tour? I mean, it all looks so interesting."

The right question: pride of ownership cheered him, stiffened him. "Well, this room, this is it. The whole works. Room for me and Tim over there and we have another helper but he's out to lunch. You want to know what's what? Over here, this table saw, just about the most important machine a woodworking shop can have. Someone told me to get the best model and I'm glad to say I did, even though at the time I didn't know a saber saw from a scroll saw from a bandsaw. And over here, the presses for veneer. The big thing here is not to panic, tighten all the clamps at once. Modern resin glues have a delayed setting time—you sure you want to hear this?—so with these glues, you've got a good ten to fifteen minutes. Time to get the whole job coated and them clamped up in strict order. And this one— watch it, don't trip on that wood—this machine, the planer. What a mistake in the beginning. I thought I could plane by hand. Me and a little elbow grease. Foolish. You wear yourself out for nothing. With this you can start with a warped or twisted board, and presto, a flat true surface. Then the sanders, and it's smooth as silk. Thrilling. And here, my workbench. Just about the most important—what's the matter?"

"A minute ago you said the table saw was the most important."

His nice diffident smile as he nodded: she had him there. "They're all important, all. The others I bought, naturally, but this workbench I made myself. My first project. See how high it is? I used to be a high-school art teacher—that is, junior high. All day I'd be bending, telling the students what was what. Too much blue in that picture. Very nice composition there. Maybe if we put the tree over here. . . . Every night I went home with a backache. So I decided, my workbench would be the right height for me."

A contented man, he drew himself up to this whole wispy height.

"And here, you can see, the first aid stuff. Power tools are great, but they can turn on you, better not forget it. The first day I worked with a power saw, it hurled pieces of timber back at my waist; back to junior high for me I thought. And that shaper over there, I was tapering legs for a small piece, I didn't pay attention when something started to rattle—it's lucky I have all my fingers. What do you do if a finger is cut off? Wrap it in ice, that's what. Get to the nearest hospital quick. Tim's laughing at me. He's right, who am I kidding? If I cut off a finger, what I'd do is faint dead away," he said with his shy candor. "And over there, you can't miss it, the dust extractor, in a shop like this, what a blessing."

"You mean, it's another most important?"

That was it: most important.

"And you showed George Theroux all this?"

"He was very interested. He asked lots of intelligent questions. A really thorough man."

She nodded. Thorough. Intelligent. Yes, indeed.

"Don't you think it odd that he never mentioned Roy Ellsworth?"

Again the blush she had noted yesterday, up the smooth cheeks and high forehead. "Maybe he didn't know. They were school friends, he and Roy. You don't tell the name of a cousin to a school friend. The way I didn't know Theroux's name."

Ah, but George knew, she thought. He came here because he knew something and wanted to find out more. She looked around, at the whitewashed walls, the shavings on the wooden floor, as if to glean from them the secret knowledge George brought with him. George, who turned out to have a remarkable talent for secrecy. Secrecy when he sat at the restaurant table with her and let slip obscure hints about a visit to Cedar Springs, secrecy even as a young boy, a young uptight boy, when he stood stubborn and unhelpful while the authorities at prep school tried to elicit from him some clues about his friend's problems.

"Mr. Elliott, I've heard that Roy got on badly with his father when he was an adolescent. Do you remember anything about that?"

"I know it was very bad." He looked over at the shaper, that machine that could betray you with the loss of a finger. "But I wasn't really tuned in then. That is, we both were busy. That is, I didn't see him much."

"Was that always true? Roy and his father not getting on?"

"Oh, no." A straight look from the pale eyes now. "Roy adored his father when he was a kid. Mostly when he and I got together, the professor would be working, but I remember once—I guess we were eight or nine—my mother and I visited them on some Caribbean Island. They had a house there—where didn't Suzanne have a house? It was not my favorite visit. Roy just wanted to be with his father. Walk on the beach with him. Pick up shells with him. Sit next to him at table. Funny. It happened so long ago, and I can still feel the envy because my eight-year-old cousin preferred his father to me."

"Well, the big change—from adoration to that terrible animosity, that really is a big change—was it about money, do you think?"

"I can't imagine," he said in his slow, scrupulous way. "The professor was always generous. Even though he never really touched Suzanne's money, he lived on his own salary—this was my mother's story—even so, a generous man."

The dust extractor obediently moved when she leaned on it. "Generous. The word you applied to Roy."

"Did I?" Once more, that provocative blush.

She looked at him, this man who criticized drawings in a junior high school before he became the owner of this impressive workshop. "Mr. Elliott, how'd you happen to get started in this business?"

Across the room, Tim had started up the planer again; the lilting voice forced itself louder. He would always be grateful to Roy, was what it said.

"It was ten years ago. My forty-fifth birthday. We always called each other for birthdays. The routine from way back. Only this time he had a special message. He said, Hey, Lee, aren't you sick of teaching those dumb bunnies how to

113

draw? What would it take to go into that woodworking you always talk about?"

She was silent. Perhaps it happened the other way. Lee Elliott said, Christ, I'm sick of teaching those dumb bunnies how to draw, if only I could go into woodworking. . . . That didn't invalidate it.

"Roy said what would I need, and I told him, well, first of all, training. All I knew was I was hooked on wood. So I hired myself out as an apprentice. The oldest living apprentice maybe in America. Tim over there, he's twenty-two, the right age for working for nothing. That is, practically nothing. Me, I had twenty-three years on him. I put in two years in this country and another in one of the great furniture development workshops in England, what an experience. Then I came back and worked six months in a place up in Maine equipped only with a radial arm saw, a router, a skillsaw, and a portable drill where they turned out forty restaurant tables a day. Then I figured I was ready to head out on my own."

The saga of Lee Elliott, master craftsman—how his voice rose and fell, his face twisted with gratified animation. Well, now she knows: press the right button and all of them talk.

"Ready! Another mistake. I didn't know beans about setting up a shop. First, I considered a place on the third floor of a loft building. Great view, airy, good light, but you try lugging those plywood strips up two flights of a narrow stairway. Then I fell for this big damp drafty barn near a river. Well, bigness is a waste, and since houses aren't damp and drafty these days, you don't want your furniture made in a place that is. And besides all that, though by then I had the skills, I hadn't the faintest idea what to do with them. In the beginning I thought in terms of small objects. Chess boards. Mirror frames shot through with inlaid colored woods. Adorable hat and coat stands."

A pause to say good-bye to Tim, who called that he was going out to lunch. "Then I hit on the design for the table and I realized that was it. One supremely beautiful object. Oh, I don't pretend I wouldn't like to keep designing. A new custom-made piece every month. But I don't kid myself. I started too late. Artists like Eames and van der Rohe, they'd been working for thirty years before they began turning out their great pieces. I can't complain. Complain, did I say! I'm a happy man. Thanks to Roy's two hundred thousand dollars I'm doing what I always wanted."

"Two hundred thousand. Wow."

"In two installments. The first was to keep me through those apprenticeship years. My mother was alive then, I'd always supported her, the money had to go for her too. And the second installment, that was to set me up. This shop and insurance and we had to bring extra power lines in; you wouldn't believe how it all mounts up. And the machines, of course. I bought them from a company going computer, someone told me to go with it and they were right. Second hand and heavy, but after a year they paid for themselves."

"All that money. Very, um, cousinly of Roy."

"Not even real cousins," he reminded her.

She thought back to that meeting yesterday, when he'd started talking about Roy's generosity and then abruptly stopped. "Mr. Elliott, did Roy's wife know about these gifts?"

"She must have known. You can't take that slice out of an income and your wife not know it."

Celia rubbed her hand along the side of a board. As he'd said, smooth as silk. "Well, did she . . . I mean . . ."

"How'd she feel about it, that what you're wondering? Oh, I don't think she was for it," he said with his wistful candor. "That is, I know for a fact she wasn't for it. It's why Roy always kept us apart. But what should I have done? Turn it down? The money to change my whole life? I don't have a family, never married, woodworking is everything to me. My great, okay, I'll say it, love."

"Mr. Elliott, I didn't mean . . ."

"Besides, they'll come into a fortune some day. Roy always said that was his father's intention. Leave them the whole lot."

She nodded, thinking, How money keeps cropping up. Money that George made clear he expected to get from his trip to Cedar Springs. Money that the Ellsworths were standing in line to inherit. Money that Roy Ellsworth gave Lee Elliott without his wife's approval.

"The truth is, I did use to worry about that money," Lee Elliott said slowly. "That is, not exactly worry. Just, you might say, wonder. That's one reason I wanted to talk to Professor Ellsworth. I'm doing all right here now. That is, not rolling in wealth, in this business it's never that. But enough advance orders to keep us on a sound footing." He looked around for a second: the proud proprietor. "So I thought, if the Ellsworth family needed something and I could maybe help out a little . . ."

"Listen," Celia burst out. "She lied to you. About the professor. That he's able to have visitors for just five minutes. Or that he sees only his family. All of it a big lie. Just the way George was lying, he must have been, when he said he wanted to buy a table with Formica on the top."

No use. She can stand here forever, among the pressers, the planers, the shapers that he cherishes, and he'll still meet her questioning thrusts with that look of patient incomprehension. He's not concealing anything. He doesn't believe there is anything to conceal. What he does believe in is the force of his own product. That and only that. Here in his workshop with the new power lines, the right size workbench, the secondhand industrial machinery, he's a man doing what he always wanted, which is to turn out one supremely beautiful object.

12

WELL, WHAT DO YOU do when a wasted day stretches behind you? A day that has opened up plenty of questions and come through with no solid help at all. You go on with your routine, that's what. It was raining when she came back to Cedar Springs and parked in front of Jefferson's, that all-purpose store where Cindy went for sunglasses and she herself hoped to buy an umbrella. Or was it too late? A man carrying a baby was leaving, and a second later, a solitary woman with a package under her arm. Celia opened the car door. That tawny head of hair, the broad shoulders in a black sweater, the long legs swinging aggressively in white slacks—Marcia, certainly. Marcia who without looking went down the street the other way.

Well, if Marcia could still get in. But when she went to the door, a man was locking it. "Closing time," he said.

"Oh, please. I'll be quick. Just an umbrella."

He pointed to the sign. Nine-thirty to six P.M.

"I know. But this awful rain. If I'm stuck without an umbrella."

He studied the rain which, with propitious timing, did suddenly come down harder, splashing on parked cars, on the slanting sidewalk, on her own unprotected shoulders. Then the door handle opened, she was inside: small-town courtesy. "Ronnie won't mind taking you," he said. "She's in the men's department, but in a pinch—Ronnie! This lady needs an umbrella."

Ronnie didn't seem to mind. Commandeered into overtime duty, she cheerfully pulled out one, then another, then two more. Then from the back of a case, still another, a blue one. This last was expensive but better built, she said. Celia should look. Good spokes, strong material.

"I don't care how expensive. If I can just have something strong, so it doesn't turn inside out in the first little wind."

"Then this blue one, it's the best. Twelve dollars—you don't mind?" Ronnie's round face wore a satisfied look; opening the umbrella in demonstration, twirling the dependable spokes, she could have been Emmy Lou's younger sister. "I like selling something that you know it will give satisfaction, but with customers you never can tell. Here you are, any price, you say, just so it's good. But a woman who was here just a minute ago, she said give me absolutely the cheapest. She didn't care how it wore or what it looked like, just it had to be cheap, cheap."

"That woman, did she have reddish brown hair and white slacks?"

"And a black sweater. She paid plenty for that sweater, believe you me. But the man's slacks and sport shirt she bought, some sleazy gray material, my own brother wouldn't wear them around the house."

"What size?"

"Large. No, extra large. Well, Miss, that rain outside, while we're at it do you maybe want a pair of boots? Miss?"

"Oh, excuse me. I was thinking." Thinking about Bernie. Bernie who from the sound of it is to be arrayed in something sporty at last. Cheap, sloppy, sleazy but undeniably sporty attire. Appropriate for someone who is in the conspiracy but not of it.

She half expected to see him in the new clothes when she

got back. Bernie in a shirt that sagged at the neck, gray pants that had to be turned up at the cuff because though he was broad, he wasn't tall; extra large would need shortening. But when she went into the lobby, there he was, bland, earnest, in the familiar business suit, and he said he was glad to see her because he hadn't wanted to leave without saying good-bye.

"You're leaving?"

"Tonight. Right now. Marcia and Jill are driving me to the bus." He nodded at Jill, who had walked over.

"Bus?" I'm not doing so well, able to come up with nothing except what Bernie says.

"Not the most comfortable ride, I grant you. But it gets there. I'll be in New York by—Just a sec." He took out the notebook and thumbed through the pages. "Eleven thirty-five. Time to still get a good night's sleep."

Then why did Marcia buy those clothes? Celia stood silent and it was Bernie who asked the questions. He wanted her address for his records. That is, unless she had objections. Not that he planned on being in Boston any time soon, but you never knew, did you, what the future would hold. And if he ran into someone nice, he didn't like to think they were out of his life completely.

He wrote with a diligent hand on a clean page of the notebook. Address and phone number, followed, she saw, by the date when he had met her and the place. And if she ever came to New York—he said it in his voice of pedantic earnestness—she must come down to see him. Lenox Paint and Hardware. Sixth Avenue in the twenties—she can't miss it. A real pleasure to have known her, he said finally.

"Oh, same here." She looked at the suitcase at his feet. Are the new slacks and shirt in there, to be worn next time he is recruited into service as a husband? Or did Marcia, when it was decided he could leave, not even bother to present them? More questions destined to remain unasked because as Jill walked away, Mrs. Ellsworth, materializing from the other side of the lobby, took her place. Teamwork. Change of guard.

"Well, there's Marcia. Time to go," Bernie said. "Goodbye again, all." More good-byes as he went. To the bird watchers, the hiker, a bellboy, a couple who'd arrived after dinner last night: Bernie being chummy, fatuous, foolish. But Marcia and Jill were ostentatiously waiting, and at last the lumbering figure made it through the lobby and out the door. Then Madeleine Ellsworth turned. "I think maybe you and I ought to have a talk."

Celia gripped the handle of her umbrella and said fine with her. Should they sit over there?

"Oh, not in here, with everyone around. Besides, I don't want my children to see us together. Let's see—still raining? No. So how about down by the brook?"

"The brook!"

"That beautiful place, you've never been there? Just go out that side door and follow the path. I'll come a different way. All right?"

Celia said all right.

"Meet you in about five minutes."

All right again as she moved toward the designated door.

And not raining, that was correct. Her toes in open sandals were wet after two steps, and bushes sent off cool sprays as she passed, but admittedly not raining. Celia walked slowly. Why did I say all right? It's not all right. I'm tired and hot and hungry. I've been sitting in a car for six hours. I want to take a shower and change my clothes and have a drink. I'm not up to fencing with a woman who so far has always outmaneuvered me.

But it was beautiful, you had to say that. She stopped at the edge of the path. She'd pictured a wide stream, a tumultuous one, like the aggressive current under the bridge on the other side of town. But this must be an offshoot, this

120

trickle that even after a rain slips in an absentminded way through the curving banks of moss and fern. Was the drama of George's death really played out against this tranquil background? She'd thought about his dying, she had a mental list of all the reasons why he wouldn't kill himself, but she hadn't pictured the act of someone else killing him. Were they already talking, he and his unknown enemy, when the shot was fired? Or had he arranged to meet someone just as she has: someone who inched quietly down from the Inn and hid behind the foliage in order to take careful aim? And if the latter, where was George standing? Here on a rock that projects far into the water? Downstream a few yards, where a line of hospitable stones enables, in fact invites, one to walk across? Or maybe he was sitting at the picnic table, being George he'd have looked with fastidious disapproval at the initials a generation of spoilers have carved in the soft wood.

In any case, he'd have been impressed. Such gentle beauty. Such unfamiliar gentle beauty. Like her, George was city bred; when the country house was still a possibility, he used to say they'd have to do some serious boning up on local fauna and flora. He wouldn't have known any more than she did what tree it was that arched over both banks, or the name of this particular species of fern, or what the white star-shaped flower was called, or whether the berries on the bush were safe for eating. She picked a berry, rolled it between her fingers, threw it in the water, which failed to register the intrusion by even a flicker of its skimming surface.

No wonder she can't see. Getting darker. If it's not raining now, the lowering clouds promise more rain any minute. Well, thanks to that courteous store manager, she has her umbrella, but what about Madeleine Ellsworth? And where is she? Five minutes?—it must be almost ten. And which way is she planning to come? Don't want my children to see us together. Why not? What is she planning to say that has to be kept from her family? *Where is she?*

If nothing happens in the next two minutes, I'll leave.

"Celia?" No umbrella, not even a scarf to put over the bushy mass of red-brown hair.

"I was beginning to give you up."

"Cindy wanted to talk to me, I had to wait till she left."

So Cindy is part of the excluded audience. "Should we sit over there?"

But they didn't. Though Madeleine nodded, though her gaze took in the scarred surface of the table, she remained standing. "We haven't been honest with each other," she said.

Well, honest. If everyone were honest, would I be here next to a brook in Cedar Springs? Celia shuffled one foot on a stone.

"For your part you didn't tell us you were George Theroux's fiancée. Or had been until the day before his death."

She looked up at the unnamed tree. "How did you know?"

"Officer Hurley told me."

A betrayal. Or isn't it? Why shouldn't Officer Hurley tell? What moral or legal strictures are there to keep him from telling? Whose side is he on?

"What difference does it make?" she asked.

"The very considerable difference that you're not the disinterested observer you led us to believe. It's obvious that anyone in your position would like to ascertain facts that point to one conclusion, and only that one, about George Theroux's death."

Oh, she's even cleverer than I thought. Didn't I tell Jason she was the clever one? "I haven't ascertained anything," Celia burst out. "If that makes you feel better."

"I'm afraid nothing about all this can really make me feel good."

Celia waited. Rain now? No, just drops shaken down from the trees by a gust of wind. "You said you were dishonest about something too."

"Not so much dishonest as reticent. Celia, I'm counting on your being a woman with reserves of tolerance." A new tone: languorous confidence.

You're mistaken, I'm not tolerant. That's true, I'm very tolerant. Which should she say?

"What I'm going to tell you I've never told anyone else. I didn't think the gist of it would be ever told to me—it's not what a woman expects to hear after she's been married a dozen years. Before marriage, yes, so she has her options, she can decide how to act. But after! Oh, believe me, when Roy told me there was no tolerance in my heart."

"Look. Shouldn't we sit down over there?" Only because I can't stand such close proximity with the steadfast gaze, the insistent features, the shining mass of hair.

"And I can't blame Roy." Impervious, the woman went on. "He was only trying to do the decent thing. He told me in the kindest way. He swore to me our marriage was the main event in his life."

"Is this really something that you . . . that I . . ."

"You're interested in George Theroux, aren't you? The George who went to school with Roy?"

"I don't get it."

"George knew, you see. Right from the beginning, Roy confided in him."

"But I thought you were talking about—"

"Another woman? Oh, my dear, I could have handled that, I would never let it worry me." She drew herself up, head erect, features sharp, as if to illustrate not just what her attractiveness was today but what it had been twenty years ago. "No, it was something else. Bisexual is what they call it. Such an ugly word. Nasty, repellent. Why would I want to be married to someone who was bisexual? But I was married to him. We'd had three children." The woman did

123

move away now, she walked a few feet along the bank. "What a mess. God, how I hated him. I thought what kind of monster is he? I wanted to smash his face. But I also loved him," the clear voice said. "And as I say, he told it in the tenderest way. He didn't blame me for being furious. He wouldn't complain if I kicked him out. But he said how much he valued me, our children, our home, our friends. That poor man, what dumb argument didn't he pull out? By the end, he even rattled off a list of other people who were also—well, like that. People in music, art, business, sports, even a famous writer. I used to say the names over and over. It was all new to me. Bisexual: I'd never even heard of the concept. I thought you had to be one thing or—the other. But there I was, age thirty-five, finding out the sordid facts of life."

A noise, but only the wind, shaking down more drops from the overhead branches. Then Celia said she still didn't understand how George came in to all this.

"Are you thinking that he also? Oh, don't worry. Not your George. No. All he was, he was the roommate. The one person who knew everything. Roy had to tell someone. In those days, a fifteen-year-old kid couldn't go to a dean and say, Hey, I love boys. Even our word for it—gay—it didn't exist. And you surely couldn't have cozy chats with a father. Not a father who was so rigid and straight and formal, who had his own high-minded ideas for his only son."

"His father never knew?"

"Once Roy dropped a hint. That was enough. The reaction was terrible. What'd I say to you in the beginning? You had to be tolerant? God knows there was no tolerance from the great professor. No tolerance, no understanding, nothing to make it easier." Madeleine was the one picking at the berries now. Pick, roll, throw, pick, roll, throw . . . an agitated reflex. "Fathers, the damage they can do. As if Roy didn't suffer enough. He wouldn't take things from his fa-

124

ther, wouldn't talk to him, wouldn't see him. Once for a whole year and a half he was so angry he—oh, it's too rotten, I don't want to talk about it."

"But the anger got over, it must have."

"It got over, all right," the woman said with a languid sigh. "As far as the old man was concerned, everything was fine. Roy was married, wasn't he? He had a wife, a family. He ran a business. That little adolescent aberration, that could be forgotten . . ."

From the back window of the Inn—that distant world—someone called for Jack. Hey, Jack, they need you in the kitchen. "But it wasn't forgotten, is that what you're trying to tell me?"

A hand went up to the bushy hair. "It's never forgotten. You know what they say about rape? The woman never gets over it, each time her husband makes love to her, the hint of horror is there? Some gesture, some involuntary position—they bring it back. That's how it was with me. A steady torment. It's why Cindy is so much younger than the others. For years, I couldn't . . . I couldn't get myself to . . ."

Is that really a sob, from that magisterial figure? Celia put out a hand and then pulled it back.

"Don't worry. I'm all right. Or rather, the marriage was all right. That's what counts, isn't it? Three quarters of marriages like ours break up—I'm giving you the facts—but we stayed together. All the times when I had my suitcase packed, I was so depressed I felt I was going mad, even when Roy said a business trip and I knew perfectly well it was just an excuse to see him . . . through it all we managed to keep it patched up."

From that vehement torrent, a single word stuck out. "Him. You knew who it was?"

When Madeleine Ellsworth stepped back, her heels dug

into the mossy bank. "Of course I knew. I thought you did too."

"How would I—" But suddenly she did know.

"Yes. Lee Elliott, of course." In the clear voice there was just an edge of triumph. The cousin who was not a cousin.

"It started—the real thing—when Lee visited Roy at that prep school. And in a sense it never stopped for Lee Elliott. A man who didn't marry, never really had anything in his life except that closet affair."

Celia pictured him: the high-school art teacher with the wispy face, diffident smile, lilting voice. Did the students laugh at him? With their offhand cruelty, did they snicker behind his back? Was that why it was so important for him to get into some other line of work?

"Roy always felt guilty. He had his life, after all. Children, friends, well, yes, marriage. That too. That's why he gave Lee money. More money, if you want to know, than we could afford. The first time, it was money we had in a trust fund to fix up the house and send Jill to college. I tried to stop him but there was nothing I could do. He said he owed it to Lee. He said Lee had always been cheated. My own child deprived; I had to sit back and take it."

Celia pulled at the curved end of a fern. "Why are you telling me all this?"

"That's what you're here for, aren't you? To find out about your Mr. Theroux's death?" Madeleine Ellsworth spoke with hard clarity.

He's changed. From "that man" to "your Mr. Theroux." "I don't see . . ."

"Come now, Celia. He succumbed, that's all. He simply succumbed to temptation. I thought he was an honorable man, but maybe that was just my dumb innocence. Or maybe it's human nature. Hold a secret long enough and eventually you'll try to get mileage out of it."

Celia walked to the edge of the water, she picked up a

stone and threw it. "George threatened to tell the professor?"

The tawny bush of hair abruptly turned. "Where did you
get that idea? The professor always knew—I thought I
made that clear. He may have put it out of his mind, deluded himself, but of course he held the knowledge. No. It
was my own children. That kind of nasty disclosure, that
was your fiancé's threat. He walked in that day and said my
children would hear everything if I didn't come through
with a payment." A thrilling scorn underlined the quiet
words. "Not any small payment either. He was going for
the big time. A sum I could get together only on the
strength of the inheritance it's presumed I'll some day get."

"They don't know about their father? Your children, I
mean?"

"They're never to know." The bleak gaze was fixed on
Celia. "It was the first thing Roy and I decided. Even before
we figured out how the two of us were going to resolve
things. Our one fixed decision. Unalterable. That none of
our children must find out." She moved a few feet away—
breathing space—but not through yet. "Especially Jerry. He
was having trouble in school then, a hyperactive eight-year-
old; of course it was no time for him to be hurt. It's the old
story, isn't it? What parents don't have some good reason
why their children rate special protection."

Bona fide drops of rain now, but neither of them moved.
"What'd you say to George?"

"You know what? I shrieked at him. I didn't stop to think
was that the right tactic or not. I just started shrieking. I
said blackmail, that's one thing. But blackmail that plays on
a man's weakness, betrays him to his own children, that's
the lowest of the low." The woman paused and looked
around, as if for the first time taking in the spot: the brook,
the trees, the bushes, the scarred table—theater for dramatic

127

death. "So when you come down to it, I guess I'm really the one to blame," she said.

"How do you figure that?"

"I shamed him," Madeleine Ellsworth said. "Made him feel rotten about himself. Any self-esteem that man might have had, I knocked it out of him. I meant it, every bitter and accusing word, but how was I to know that because of it he'd come down here and put a bullet through his heart?"

13

"SO THAT'S HOW IT ended," she said to Jason. "The way every monologue she's addressed to me has always ended. George stands in that heavenly spot next to the brook and shoots himself."

"But in her version the shooting isn't because he's been rejected by you."

"No," she agreed wearily. She's entitled to be weary. It's taken her almost half an hour to report to him on the long day. Every detail of that tormented saga from Madeleine Ellsworth, the unavailing visit to Lee Elliott, even the bizarre trivia of Marcia's having bought cheap slacks and a shirt for Bernie at a time when he was already jotting into the notebook the time his bus was due to arrive in New York. A lot to go over by phone—yes, she's weary, all right.

Jason asked if Madeleine Ellsworth had sounded convincing.

"Oh, yes. Very."

"And her story is surely a persuasive one."

"Persuasive. Yes."

"Also, as you tell it, a lot of questions explained. Just about every question, in fact. Why George told you that when he came back from Vermont he might be able to swing the house. Why Roy paid out all that money for Lee

Elliott's start in woodworking. And of course why the adolescent Roy went through the anguish of that traumatic period with his father."

"Right. Everything neatly explained. Also," she added, "it leaves all of them in the clear."

"I don't get it."

"Well, Madeleine could not have killed George because she was playing bridge. That's the one sure fact the police have to hold on to. Three people testify that she never left the table between the critical hours of two and four. So the only one with an authentic alibi is now also the only one who had reason to find George a menace."

"I'd forgotten that. God, that marriage, a wretched story, isn't it?"

"Very."

"Must have taken courage on her part to tell it to you."

She pictured the magisterial features under the reddish-brown mass of hair. "Oh, she's courageous, all right."

"Can't have been easy, living with Roy all those years."

"I guess not." Celia shifted the receiver to the other ear.

"And it's true that people in that situation can feel it absolutely imperative that their children never find out. No matter how mature and big-hearted those children seem to be."

"I guess so."

"Celia, you sound tired."

Tired! Beat. Dead. Out of it. "Oh, well . . ."

"Celia, listen. I know it's not the slam-bang solution you were hoping for. Definitive proof that one of them slipped down there with a gun and did him in. But it does seem to be—"

"Yes. Convincing." She paused. Some people were going by outside, calling to Hal, Hal you idiot, just wait up, and she was silent until their noisy hilarity had passed. "Unless, of course, the whole story is a fake," she said then.

"But you said—"

"That she sounded persuasive. I know. She's a wholly

130

persuasive woman, also one with bottomless reserves of ingenuity and brilliance, and her story has great plausibility. Agreed. I just say it's possible that she made the whole thing up." And when he didn't answer—"Jason, it's a cinch that she guessed correctly where I went today. That meeting with Lee Elliott she did her best to forestall last night. And once she knew I was with him . . ."

"But you said he told you nothing."

"He told me about the money. An inexplicable two hundred thousand dollars from a man who at that point could ill afford to give it. Inexplicable, that is, until she cooked up a dazzling explanation."

Another speculative pause. "Celia, all this must have been painful to her. Painful, crushing, demeaning. It's not, after all, the kind of disclosure a woman relishes having to make to a stranger. So why would she go in for that kind of purposeful degradation if it weren't true?"

She looked out on the green, where the small figures on the path had again put up their umbrellas. "Because she wants me to quit. She doesn't like me snooping around. She's afraid of what I'll find out."

Another jolly crowd had breezed by outside before Jason's words came over the phone. "Celia, that snooping, as you call it, has been tremendous. You've sized up that family, got people to talk, followed every lead—no one could have done it better. But the possibility does remain that it's finished, you've shot your bolt."

She leaned back in the cushioned chair. She might have known it would come. A time when these nightly talks would pall; he'd figure he'd heard enough about Marcia, Bernie, Cindy, Jill. He's never seen them, after all; for all her efforts to paint them in vivid colors, he can't envision the alert eyes, the censoring gaze that goes around the table, the conspiratorial glow. They don't at once fascinate and repel him.

"So what's your advice?" She said it coldly, a sarcastic

nonquestion, but he came through with a serious answer. She should lie low. Not try to interview anyone. Cut her losses. Just . . . well . . .

"Do my job with the professor?"

It was what she was there for, he reminded her.

The job she took only so she could track down George's murderer. A job, moreover, she's not fit for, that doesn't in the least call on the skills she's perfected over the years, that's keeping her in a place where after the first brush with all this bucolic beauty she doesn't particularly want to be.

And yet she likes it. The funny thing is she really does like it. She didn't believe she would at first. Benjamin Franklin, Edward Gibbon, why should their inability to come clean about those distant childhoods be anything to her? But the whole subject has grown on her; she's addicted; she can't wait to find out who the next set of youthful heroes and heroines will be, and how their stories will at once embody and counter the absolutes about child rearing that the authorities have set up.

And the professor is in something of the same boat. He started this—little by little it's become clear—out of concern about his own family. Why were they such deadbeats, what did it have to do with him, how much could he blame on outside pressures, but he's thrown himself into it; every day he delves into that prodigious memory and finds examples that glitter on their own. Between the two of them, a book is taking shape.

"We missed you," Les said when she walked in next morning.

She said honestly the feeling was mutual. Then she stopped. That yummy smell—what is it?

"Muffins. Arnie makes them. Want to try one? Come on in. My brother Arnie, Celia Sommerville."

Standing next to the kitchen table, they were alike: the same ruddy faces, clear blue eyes, open smiles. And the same eager pleasure in talking. Muffins, Arnie's specialty.

He brings some for the professor whenever he makes a batch. The only thing Arnie can really make—Arnie, shut up—if she wants to know the truth. When they open their restaurant in two years, Arnie will do the buying, the general managing; it'll be Les at the stove stirring the sauces. And their father, he'll be walking around, eyeing the ladies, giving the homey touch a restaurant up here can use.

"Two years, did you say?"

"That's the deal," Les said. "I stay with the professor that long, he sees to it we have enough to set up in business. . . . Hey, you didn't taste one."

"Thanks."

Blueberry on this side, Arnie explained, over there whole wheat. The professor goes for whole wheat, but she should feel free to sample both.

She bit into the flaky crust, gave an admiring sigh.

"Come over some day; I make six other kinds. And my father would like it; he loves pretty women, doesn't get to see enough of them. Know where we live?"

She said she did. And when the two faces leaned forward expectant, she said it had seemed beautiful, house and barn nestling together at the foot of that little incline. "But a truck was honking behind me, I couldn't really look."

She should come again—they both said it. They'll give her a proper tour. Especially their father. He's wild about the place, even though his health these days doesn't allow him to really work on it. But it's his dream place, what keeps him going, thank the good lord they have it.

Oh, she doesn't blame Professor Ellsworth for wanting them around, these young men with their cheery manners, their filial concerns, their candid enthusiasms. A tonic.

And he did look well when she went up. More about *The Mill on the Floss* was what he said. Specifically, more about Maggie, that little girl with the impetuous nature, the good quick mind, the valiant impulses, even the need for affection—none of these attributes suitable for an age when prompt submission to parents was still what the arbiters of child culture required.

"I once collected a sheaf of reviews from magazines of the eighteen-sixties. I think if you look in the portfolio on that second shelf? . . . You have them? Now, my dear, if you'd like to read them."

She would never get used to the idea that her voice was being recorded; she read in her usual cautious monotone. "'Maggie is possessed of a strong unsatisfied erring youth.' 'Her childhood is without the development of regulating principles.' 'Her temptations to vanity and many other faults are wild and fierce.' Oh, here's another. It says, "that little doll she sticks pins in, her way of getting rid of her anger, they call this an exercise in 'unnatural ferocity.'"

He nodded. "Yes, my dear. You get the point. An intriguing one. According to the magazines that people of those days were reading, that little girl we consider so bright and volatile is one they find imprudent and wildly irresponsible. And the thing to remember is, George Eliot agrees. She may draw Maggie with sympathy, but make no mistake, she agrees with the experts. She knows that the wonderful spirited Maggie is not all that wonderful and has no business showing such spirit. Even more, she knows that lack of control in childhood leads inevitably to a mindless abandon in adulthood. Which is why, as we remember, that abandon has to be paid for the hard way."

All as usual. Eloquent, instructive, sharp. Except after a few minutes she realized the sharpness had modulated to a quavery murmur. "She was lucky, George Eliot. All authors are lucky in a sense. In position, as we humans are not, to dole out whatever punishments they think are due. Exact whatever retribution is appropriate. And then live comfortably with themselves in the conviction that justice has been done."

She looked up startled. She'd let her mind wander while he went on about Maggie Tolliver. Maggie, whose unapproved high spirits in childhood lead with implacable steps to a watery doom when she grows up. But here he was talking about something not related to Maggie at all. Or at least related only in the most oblique way. And talking in a voice of such vague melancholy. Such a bleak expression in the half-closed eyes.

But then he pulled at the blanket and with his usual placidity looked up. She should run along now. Next session they would move up some twenty-five years. The children in *Turn of the Screw*.

She ran along back to the Inn. Her only destination from now on. Lie low: Jason's orders. You inquire at the desk for mail and talk in the lobby with the bird watchers about the scarlet tanager they saw this morning, and then, in the sudden sunshine that breaks through a bank of clouds, you go out on the porch. More activity here. In this exemplary hotel, maids knock on the door early to say can they make the beds, and carts with dirty linen are out of sight by ten A.M., but outdoor work goes on all day. Three men at it now: one watering the geraniums, one clipping the grass that springs up disallowed on the flagstone walk, one pulling weeds from the flower bed around the flag pole. And besides them, two men in shorts taking suitcases out of a car—an animated landscape. So why does she keep seeing that woman who stood with her vehement words and stubborn pose next to the brook?

Maybe Jason is right: some defect in me that I don't trust her, I put up all these obstacles to belief. Or maybe it's another effect of this whole business of trying to play detective. A woman comes to you with a credible story, one that's no fun for her to relate and that coincides perfectly, moreover, with the character of the people involved, and what happens? You dismiss it. You feel it's incumbent on you to summon up a steely and offended resistance. Instead of welcoming an account that provides a neat solution to all the problems, you think how smart you are to catch out the neatness.

Her thoughts left her shaken; when she saw Marcia and Jill standing a few feet away, she walked over. Simple courtesy.

Jill responded in kind. This old sleigh, so adorable, imagine someone thinking of that idea, a sleigh painted and filled with flowers. In fact, this whole hotel, the way they've kept the spirit of an old building without sacrificing all the, you know, comforts. And the town. Too quaint, you think at first, but some really creative people. A store two down from the movie house, this woman who makes tiny glass ornaments. The kind you can paste on a window; Jill is not going to leave without buying some. And next door to that, the leather store. But not the bulky stuff you might expect, very delicate and original, you wouldn't believe. . . . On and on, the inconsequential talk of three women standing together on a hotel porch on a sunny morning. As if without having been told they understand that through their mother's intervention Celia Sommerville has been removed from the category of enemy, it is no longer necessary to try to score points with her.

When Cindy came out, it continued. The leather store?—awesome. Cindy knows it well. For sure. There's a little tan jacket she wants, isn't going to leave till she has it.

"How much?" Jill asked.

"Four hundred."

"Four hundred dollars for a leather jacket that you can't even wear in the winter!"

"The ones with hand painting, they're more."

The store had sweaters too, Marcia offered in her elder sister conciliatory voice. But Cindy wasn't having any. She wanted the jacket.

"Cindy, come on. You can't ask Mom for that kind of money, you know perfectly well."

Cindy hunched her shoulders; in deference to the warm

morning, she had left off the sweatshirt. "It's all right for you two, you get out, have your own life. You don't have to hang around in this dump day after day."

Dump! Marcia looked quickly around, but no other guests within earshot. "Relax, baby. Only three days more. Besides"—her voice still slightly tutorial—"as if we didn't hang around too."

"You weren't hanging last night," Cindy said, and on her face Celia noted the same smirking look as when her friends had come over to ask Jill for the autograph. "You put a hundred and eighty miles on the car."

Jill waved a negligent hand: Cindy was crazy, she said.

"Don't deny it. Exactly one eighty. Jerry and I drove to that ice cream place yesterday, I noticed the speedometer was at twenty nine, nine, nine, nine. You know, four nines changing to zeroes. And this morning it's at thirty one eight oh, I looked in."

Jill raised her eyebrows as if in despair at one so callow as to look in a car to check mileage.

"And that stink. Jeez. I never smelled anything like it. That back seat, like someone poured a whole bottle of whiskey over it."

There was just an instant when Marcia and Jill looked at each other, those large eyes exchanged a message. Then Marcia took her sister by the shoulders. "Cindy, baby, listen. We . . . okay we picked up a couple of guys last night after we left Bernie at the bus stop. Not so smart, but we did it. So then we drove around, one bar, then another, all those miles, wow, we didn't realize."

"And one of them did spill his whiskey," Jill said. "Pickups, not so nice."

"I swear, you two, you make me sick," Cindy said.

A man started walking over as though, in hotel-porch camaraderie, he planned to join them, but someone called to him, he changed course. "Cindy. Don't tell Mom," Marcia said. "You hear! She'd go off her rocker just when . . . Really don't tell."

Celia tactfully kept her gaze on the flowers, but she realized Marcia wasn't trying to exclude her; her role as audience seemed to be taken for granted. "I'll buy you that jacket if you don't tell," Marcia went on. "The leather one. Cindy? . . ."

"Well . . ."

"This afternoon," Jill put in. "First thing, we'll go pick it up. Cindy, that okay?"

Cindy gave her sullen nod. But it was a pact, Celia knew. No one had to say, swear, or promise, or hope to die. Relief was stamped on both the large, smooth faces: Cindy wouldn't tell, they could trust her. A family used to dealing in secrets.

14

"SO, CELIA, HAVING SEEN that it is still incumbent on children to jump in obedience to their parents, in *The Turn of the Screw* we see why. Because they are not trustworthy. As sexual creatures, they are unreliable. Those sexual proclivities: that is the crux of it. The reason the nineteenth-century child is loved but not accredited, observed without being understood, destined to provide salvation while needing always to be saved from his own worst impulses.

"As to what exactly these impulses are, the nineteenth-century novelist is obviously not authorized to expose them. Henry James does not expose them to the light of day either; what he does—it's an amazing trick—is to palm them off as the material of a young woman's nightmare. With his extraordinary craft, he transfigures them. What does this nightmare material consist of? Why does the governess suppose the dead servants and the children are trying to get together? What do they want to do? What did they allegedly do before? After all the hints and loaded intimations, of what practices do the young boy and the groom, or the girl and the ex-governess, stand accused?

"James never says; the hints are all. The groom Quint was much too free—not just with the boy, but with everyone. Is a pushy egalitarianism thus suggested? Hardly. Rather, what went on—and again, Celia, my usual request:

be sure to check the quotes before typing them in the final copy—what went on were 'things terrible and unguessable and that sprang from dreadful passages of intercourse in the past.' It is the language of all the nineteenth-century experts on children, meant to intimidate but not required to inform."

She sat back as the voice on the tape went on, while at the other end of the phone she could hear Jason's voice giving little murmurs of interest and amazement. He had called around nine and said why hadn't she called. Well, she'll be glad to call, now it's tacitly settled between them that this and only this is what he wants to hear: the words of Professor Ellsworth. Their mode of communication from now on: a tape.

"Wonderful," he said, when she turned the machine off. Yes.

"I've been teaching that book for a dozen years and I never thought of it in quite that way before."

"He was very good," she agreed.

"And to think he does it all from memory, no checking of notes or texts."

More agreement.

"As for being able to quote, quote accurately from what I remember, what a feat."

Um, hmm.

"Celia, anything new with the family?"

She gripped the chair. He doesn't mean it, he's being courteous. What he thinks is courtesy. Indulging her quaint fears. Paying lip service to her imaginary problems. But he's not the least interested; the last thing she's going to do is come clean about the uncertainties that assail her.

"That's finished," she said, "I don't even have dinner with them, that exercise in dutiful hospitality ended last night."

"How'd that happen?"

She explained: Bernie had decided to leave, which called

for Jill and Marcia to drive him to the bus stop some ten miles away, which meant there was not the usual convivial gathering at dinner. "Just the mother and Jerry and that sulky Cindy; by the time I came down the three of them were on dessert. So from now on I sit at my old solitary table. What I want and I'm sure they want."

"Bernie left?"

"And Jill and Marcia had themselves a night out after they took him." Despite her intentions, she heard herself giving the details. "They picked up a couple of guys and did a tour of roadside bars that went on for hours, all of them probably stinking drunk."

"How do you know all this?"

"Because Cindy, that perennial troublemaker, checked the mileage, which was a hundred and eighty miles ahead of what it should have been, and she also smelled the back seat, which seems to have been the receptacle for a spilled bottle of whiskey. So what could her sisters do except admit? With a proviso. Cindy, baby, don't tell mama."

Why'd she start this? She's used to giving a full report, she'll have to work at getting out of the habit. "Anyhow, none of it's my concern," she pointedly added, and even more curtly she said goodnight, she had to go.

She doesn't have to. She has nothing in the world to do. She doesn't even feel sleepy. Hotels. They can be an all-day picnic, a fun fair, a ticket to another world, but they can also be a trap, a setting that gives you no chance to work off the restlessness. She looked around the pretty room. At home, there would be something needing repair or restoration: a curtain hem undone, a shelf paper torn, a box of old letters waiting to be sorted out—anything to keep the unease at bay. Nine-thirty. She can go down to the lobby and look through the manuals on fishing and mountain climbing. Or she can go out on the porch, where that nice father and son are always looking for conversation. Or presumably, since she is also possessed of a car and certain indubitable assets, she can go for the option that Jill and Marcia chose last night.

In the end she read and went to sleep late, but not late enough. Tossing, throwing off a blanket and pulling it on again, she must have dreamed of being back home because she thought she heard fire engines, those strident noises that in the city are an accustomed counterpart to any night's sleep but strike an anomalous note in the country's invincible stillness.

It was fine weather next morning, the sun hitting the geraniums and the men already clipping, weeding, cutting: Cedar Springs Inn stage set. And more glories as she walked along the ridge, noting the clarity of the distant mountains, and the companionable cluster of finches on the overhead wires, and the pattern made by the white fences as they met and crossed and separated again on the lower fields. Even the professor's garden sparkled. It received the perfunctory care of any garden not used by its owner—no annuals planted in the beds, no water in the green-stained bird bath, surely no arrangements of rustic furniture on the lawn—but the grass still held the dew and some blue flower that must be a leftover from an earlier era had nudged itself upright against a wall. Celia rang the bell. If Arnie is here with muffins this morning, he won't have to ask me twice.

Madeleine opened the door. "Good morning, Celia. I thought it might be time for you to come."

"Nine-thirty," she said. "I always come at nine-thirty." She stood on the stone walk. What am I doing defending myself? How does she manage it?

"He'll be glad to see you. Come in," Madeleine added, because Celia had not moved.

From the hall, she could see into the bright kitchen. Les's kitchen. Why isn't he there? And why, at an hour when she usually sits in the dining room having her second cup of coffee, is this woman standing next to the stairs with a dish towel in one hand and an ambiguous smile on her lips?

142

"An accident," Madeleine said. "Dreadful fire last night. It demolished the barn. Lester's father's barn, that is."

"My God."

"It hadn't been a working barn for many years, but there you are, all that flammable stuff, wooden implements and straw and what not. Country people," she said. "Sentiment counts more than practicality."

"The barn . . ." That thin sound, that's her voice. A voice bearing no relation to her mental image of a large red building, ponderous, handsome, standing in harmonious conjunction with a small pretty house. Did fire engines have trouble navigating that incline, those engines that were not after all the stuff of dreams?

". . . didn't hesitate, of course," Madeleine said. "Three in the morning, but I could understand Lester's wanting to be with his injured father. Waking Jerry, that was maybe the hardest job, but once he understood he was up like a shot. That boy, what a speed demon when there's an emergency."

A few words got through. Injured . . . emergency . . . Jerry. Jerry, whose footsteps it must be she is hearing in the hall upstairs.

"I did get a little sleep after we came. No beds ready, of course, but that couch in there, it's not uncomfortable. But Jerry didn't close his eyes. He thought, suppose his grandfather wakes up. Jerry, there you are. Everything all right?"

"Ship shape." Jerry was carrying a tray which he deposited in the kitchen before joining them again. "He's a little off his feed, but he ate the cereal."

"Jerry's a good nurse," his mother said with a little chuckle, as if describing the feat of a six-year-old.

Jerry didn't deny the encomium, but his sallow face didn't take on any special look of pleasure either. Maybe Celia would like a cup of coffee, he suggested, and pointed to the kitchen. That large airy kitchen which he had appropriated.

"Oh, no. No thanks."

"Should we go up then? Oh, one more little thing. Just as well not to talk to the professor about what happened," Madeleine said. "He knows the bare facts, of course, but no use distressing him further."

I can't very well talk about what I don't know myself. But as she was by now walking up the stairs, with Madeleine Ellsworth beside her, she didn't say this. Nor did she say, Why are you coming with me, this is a private hour between me and the professor, I would really rather you stayed downstairs.

Professor Ellsworth gave his usual mild smile when they walked in. "Good morning, my dear. Perhaps you wouldn't mind closing that window a little. . . . Now, where were we? Yes. James had found in *The Turn of the Screw* the tactic for delineating the perils of child sexuality while at the same time not delineating them. The most conspicuous of these perils concerns what was then euphemistically called self-abuse—a practice against which the child-care experts conducted open warfare right through the century. If the heroine of our story accepts the menace, she also sticks with the instructions for handling it. Constant surveillance was the watchword for anyone who took care of children; exhorted to guard the codes, an adult was plainly expected to keep an eye. The governess is an able practitioner of such vigilance. As she says proudly, in a quote I trust I'm getting right but that Celia will submit to the customary check: 'The children know my inexorable, my perpetual society. . . . I had all but pinned the boy to my shawl.' But the real danger, of course, lurks at night. Sleep with Flora obviously; it is an arrangement of which the health authorities would have approved. But also all that sitting by the beds, pulling back of sheets, keeping on of lights, bending over for the unannounced caress—no chance of hanky panky here. In one of his moving little pleas, Miles say he simply wants her to let him alone. But she won't. She can't. If the

144

mechanics of surveillance are sanctioned by her era, they also are gratifying to her being; she exactly embodies—it is James's triumph—the urge to probe, to pry, that is the hallmark of the repressed personality."

There they are, the usual transcendent sentences coming out with the studied perfection of a lecture. But it's not a lecture he delivers here twice a day. Or not just a lecture. It's an exchange, a tutorial, an exercise in reminiscence, a therapeutic session. Maybe a therapeutic session most of all, in which she works through some problems and he works through some problems and each gives unspoken comfort to the other.

No comfort this morning, in fact to Celia's mind an air of extreme discomfort. The visitor sat very still with an expression of careful interest, and she surely didn't interrupt or advance an opinion. However, she was here. Occupying a chair. Breathing the air. An intruder. Maybe if Professor Ellsworth would offer some acknowledgment of her presence. We have company this morning. Or, Our little session is enlarged today. Or even, Perhaps I should explain to Madeleine the ground we've covered so far. But no. Not a word, a gesture, as if Madeleine's calm assumption that she belongs here is her father-in-law's assumption as well.

Maybe this afternoon she won't be here; it was what the woman said when they went downstairs. "We have to take it step by step, Jerry and I. Play it by ear. See what's going to happen."

"I don't really understand what happened in the first place."

"A shocker for us too. Should we go in here?" Here was the living room, a place with large windows and a great stone fireplace, but still with a look of being dark, damp, stuffy, dreary. The way a room gets to look when it's underutilized.

What happened, Madeleine said, was a fire in the middle of the night. Those fires, who could explain them? A carelessly thrown cigarette, a spark that's been smoldering for hours. In conjunction, of course, with all that ill-advised straw. But no one would've been hurt had Lester's father stayed where he was. Where he belonged. In the house, which was never threatened. But a sick man, he lost his head and ran outside; in his panic he went too near the burning barn. At which point Lester's brother—"

"Arnie."

The level gaze went over her. "I believe that's his name. He went to his father's aid, and though a beam from the burning barn didn't exactly fall on them, it fell close enough so the brother's hand was burned."

The hand that yesterday was holding out a tray of muffins.

"As for Lester's father, a man with a cardiac condition, he may not be in as bad shape as they say. Hospitals exaggerate. In which case Les will be back and Jerry and I can retire."

Celia looked around. Heavy couch, bear rug, coffee table where no one these days stretches their feet or reaches for a drink. Once people tramped boisterously in here, shaking snow off their boots, blowing on icy fingers, calling out that they were absolutely starved. "Isn't there some woman who used to work for them, she still lives here in Cedar Springs?"

"Mattie Haines." Again the judgmental gaze. "But she's seventy years old, past seventy, and overweight. I wouldn't dream of turning over to her the sole care for my father-in-law's meals. Which reminds me. If I want his lunch to be ready on time." Madeleine buttoned her cardigan. "A casserole, I thought. Something innovative, after Lester's good but routine meals."

Her dismissal. She went briskly down the path, producing for whatever eyes might be watching the walk of one on her way to pressing but pleasant pursuits. But nothing pleasant about what she did next, which was to get her car

146

and drive out to that site near the covered bridge where route 84A crosses the main road. Then she asked herself why. What did she expect to find? The fire engines must have made their way down that small incline, but a rope tied to trees on either side of the driveway effectively blocked it; she was one of a crowd of ten or twelve forced to stand above while they gaped at charred beams, scorched trees, great muddy holes where the fire hoses had played. Did the front siding give way first, exposing to an ill man's shocked gaze the straw and wooden implements that Madeleine had said it was folly for him to keep? Or did the roof go off in a great swoosh, allowing the trapped heat to find its way out in a swirling cloud of smoke and blazing debris? "Son of a bitch," the man next to her said, taking off his hat. Silence followed this until another man tugged at his ear and said in a sour mumble that he heard the police found a tin for gasoline; he wouldn't be surprised; they'd always wanted to get their money out of this place. But he was plainly a minority. An unfavored minority. Half a dozen voices snarled at him. Shut up with that, Harry. None of that talk, Harry. Those two boys, known 'em since they was born, they would never. "So how'd it happen if someone didn't set it?" Harry asked in a last defiant gasp, but the surrounding faces held only unfriendly scorn, and after a minute he slunk away.

She left too, defeated in a different way. And defeated, finally, when she called the hospital, because not being accredited—"No, just a friend"—she was put off with the standard formula: guarded but stable.

Guarded: So that faint hope, that the afternoon visit would be different, must be stilled. But in fact when she and Madeleine took their seats, and the window had been adjusted that critical half an inch, and she switched on the tape recorder, and the lined face turned on them his mildly quizzical look, there did turn out to be a difference.

"I guess you've noticed, my dear. Lester gone, my

147

daughter-in-law and grandson aboard. I feel for Lester, but old age is selfish, I can't help the very real pleasure for myself. One's own family taking care, attuned to the special wishes, geared for the extra indulgences, prepared to give the unaccustomed treats—it does set one up. And of course a new set of discerning ears—what every teacher once in a while needs for inspiration.

"So, then, a new book this afternoon. *What Maisie Knew*. Still Henry James, but another child. A child who finds out the hard way that she is unloved. First Mama makes plain, after the divorce, that she exacts the six-month visit with Maisie only as a device to torment her husband; then it appears that this gentleman has a similar rationale; then the pretty governess who adores her little charge turns out to adore her only as she provides a façade of propriety for the liaison with Papa; and finally the beloved Sir Claude, who is Mama's current husband, divulges one morning over rolls and coffee that he too has joined the club. What Maisie knows by the end is that she is a pretext for the game— whatever dirty little game at the moment is being played."

Celia sat stiffly. Extra indulgences . . . special wishes . . . unaccustomed treats. She'd thought this morning that if he would acknowledge the new presence, it would help. But now he has acknowledged it, and she wants to weep. It's nothing personal, she can tell herself over and over it's nothing personal, but what she feels is nothing more or less than simple rejection. That emotion with the power to activate the memory of past rejections and bear their cumulative weight. Sitting here in the breezy room, she's the audience whose discerning ears are not sufficient to provide inspiration, and she is also the sixteen-year-old whose date fondled her in the back of his car and then failed to call her again, she is the recipient of a letter that someone else has got the job, she is the long-ago wife whose husband announced with rueful pride that he was sleeping with someone else.

"Nothing is spared this little girl. . . ." Still going on. "Maisie's father tells her with his pleasant confidentiality that her mother loathes her, and her mother, equally succinct, explains that her father wishes she were dead. No wonder in the end she chooses Mrs. Wix. Mrs. Wix who on every count is a grotesque, a ridiculous old woman. But what she wants is for Maisie to be happy, Maisie's happiness, indeed, is her sole aim."

Finished at last. Celia took her tape recorder and went to the door. Another communal exit, Madeleine telling her about the innovative casserole that beats Lester's routine meals? No, the woman is bending over Professor Ellsworth, perhaps offering one of the special indulgences or confiding how much her discerning ears enjoyed the talk. Family! She went out into the wide hall. She always walks straight down, but now she took a minute to study the shape of the house. Two houses, really. This part, that must have been the original, and another segment, maybe added on, as the custom was, after fifty or seventy-five years. The servants must have slept in that other part that goes off on a diagonal from this main hall, while the professor and his errant wife Suzanne had the suite the professor now inhabits. As for the young Roy, doubtless this room across the hall. Presumably Madeleine will sleep in it tonight, but as of now no suitcase on the bed, no clothes in the open closet. Celia walked in. A large airy room, with one window opening on the back lawn and another looking out on the driveway that runs along the side of the house. An Ellsworth car parked down there now—the one that had added to it one night one hundred and eighty miles plus a reprehensible stink? The door she has noticed in the kitchen must open onto that driveway—trust these old houses to have sensible arrangements for bad weather and heavy loads.

"What do you think you're doing!" Madeleine Ellsworth,

with the large features twisted into a wholly new look of ferocity.

"I was just . . . such an interesting house plan, I was curious to see what—"

"Get moving! Just move your ass away from that window. Go!"

Well, when someone yells at you like that, you don't wait to find out what's going on, you move fast. But Celia has in fact found out something. That underneath the calmly judicious speech and imperturbable gaze Madeleine carefully cultivates, there's a shrieking temper waiting to get out.

15

OVER HER SOLITARY dinner she made her decision. Between salad and coffee her mind made up: simple as that. And she knew it was right because there were no doubts or second thoughts or reappraisals. Only, as she left the dining room and walked out to the porch, a bland detachment. As if she were gone already.

Detachment: it makes everything easy. You don't get the usual thrill at the final burst of pink cloud sinking below the distant bell tower, but on the other hand, you can pick up the pamphlet someone has left on your chair, and as if it were interesting reading, go over for the third time the account of how the early settlers made maple syrup.

And still detached when the bellboy brought a woman over and said, "Maybe Miss Sommerville can help you." A woman with small eyes, splotchy skin, a pinched face, who pulled at the skirt of her dark blue dress while she spoke. She was looking for Bernie Lenox, was what she said.

"Bernie?"

"Do you know where he is?"

"Oh, listen, you don't want me. See those two women over there?" Because Marcia and Jill had just come out on the porch. "That's who you want."

But if the newcomer wanted them, she seemed unable to

do anything about it. She stared at the two figures in their sweaters and slacks, their air of voluptuous vigor, and she seemed to shrink into a scowling immobility. Celia finally called to them. Marcia! Jill! Then she prodded the woman. Go on and ask them.

The woman made a great effort. She was sorry. She didn't want to bother them. Maybe the whole thing a mistake. But she couldn't help being worried. He was usually such a stickler about time. Let him say he would meet you at a certain hour and there he was on the button. So when he didn't turn up at the store.

"He?" Marcia raised a hand to the nest of hair.

"Didn't I say? Bernie. Bernie Lenox."

How could they not know, Celia thought. That gauche, long-winded, apologetic explanation—how could they be in any doubt that it must concern Bernie?

What about him, they asked.

"Then you do know him. They told me at the desk . . ."

What did they tell her? And will it embarrass Marcia and Jill, who have paraded Bernie before Celia as a husband? No, nothing embarrasses Marcia and Jill; those large serene faces are embarrassment-proof. Besides, it occurs to her that the husband myth has been gradually fading; every time one or another of them at table met Bernie's heavy pedantry with their jovial contempt, it was as if they said, Forget that husband business, it's all played out, in front of Celia it's no longer necessary to dissemble.

Marcia's voice now held the same dismissive note. "I don't get it. We drove him to the bus stop two nights ago—Jill, what time was that?"

Jill didn't remember. Bernie was in charge, he scheduled it. Whatever time he told them, that's when they got him there.

"He never came home," the woman blurted out.

"Very sorry, Miss . . . um . . ."

She put her hand to her face as if to cover its splotches. Then she said her name was Janet Arbib and she was Bernie's business partner. Sort of partner. Bernie owned two thirds of the hardware and paint store, and she owned one third.

"Maybe he came home and just never made it down to the store," Jill suggested—the kind of unkind suggestion, Celia thought, Cindy might have come out with.

But Janet Arbib shook her head. She'd been calling and calling his apartment, and no answer.

Or maybe a bus accident?—But this too had been checked out.

For a minute they all were silent, joint spectators at the view. Sunsets faded fast; by now the bell tower, the steeples, the roof tops were colorless shapes against a darkening sky. Marcia's hand went out to tilt a rocking chair back and forth. "How did you know he was up here anyhow?"

"I finally went to his apartment. This morning, I mean. I found the name—Cedar Springs Inn—on a card on his desk." A blush rose up the splotched cheeks to the edge of her thin brown hair, and Celia thought, Not just a business partner, not just that at all.

Then she saw the mocking slant of Marcia's mouth, and she knew Marcia was thinking the same thing. A natural thing to think, and one calculated to give rise, in a natural way, to more unkindness. "Bernie's a big boy," Marcia said. "Just because we left him at the bus stop, that doesn't mean. . . . Maybe he changed his mind. Maybe he took a different bus. Maybe he decided the hell with it, he wasn't ready to come home."

Janet Arbib worked at this, eyes blinking, hand rubbing one side of the pinched nose. "No. He had to be home, he wanted to be. Thing is—well, he owed me money. I . . . I've laid out for the rent the past three months. Things haven't been going so well at the store, You know, it sometimes happens like that, all your hard work but still you get in the red."

"You mean, the store's a losing proposition?" Jill spoke with easy triumph.

As if realizing her mistake, Janet Arbib stood with shoulders hunched, gaze fixed downward. Then she tried again. Things were going to be different. Bernie was getting some money, he said so. They were going to be able to enlarge into some space next door.

"Man with money in his pocket, you can't always tell. Lots of times they go getting ideas." That smirk on Jill's face—the same expression Cindy wore when she brought over her two friends and it was Jill being discomfited. Now the recipient of the look is a woman in a cheap blue dress without any particular capacity to fight back.

"When Bernie told me good-bye, he said he'd be in New York at eleven-thirty-five." Celia surprised herself by getting into it. "He sounded as if he meant it."

All at once, a firm voice from Janet Arbib. Maybe the unexpected support from Celia had stiffened her, told her she didn't have to keep cringing. "We've been planning it for months. An added four hundred square feet, that doesn't sound like so much, but it could change everything. A customer walks in, they don't want to wait while you climb on a ladder, go rummaging around. You need to have everything out in the open, so you can see it and they can see it. Speedy service, that's how you beat out the competition. That and being able to give the right advice." Anger gave her a whole new authority; she was the source from which the right advice would emanate. Standing behind the counter, explaining how to get rid of mold on the bathroom tiles, or why the newly painted ceiling had developed cracks, or what was needed to remove the eight old layers of wallpaper, she would look not scrawny but resolute. The customers' friend.

154

Only now she's at the mercy of Jill and Marcia, who manage to drop innuendos while they express sympathy, make clear their belief that a man with money in his pocket is going to think twice about coming home to a girl with splotchy skin and a poor pinched face.

Well, Celia thought, not my problem. Not remotely my problem. Detachment, how fragile it is, and how you have to work at keeping it intact. She murmured something about a phone call and said good night, and she'd made it through the lobby and over to the stairs when the voice caught up with her. "Please. Wait a second."

She stood with one foot on the second step.

"I know what they think." Janet, eyes flashing, voice ringing. "He walked out on me. He owed me money and business was no good and this was his big chance. But they're wrong. You know why?" She stopped, but only because a family of four was coming down the stairs. "Because he loves that store. More than anything. He would never leave it."

Another pause: the bird watchers, with pleasant nods, walked by.

"Besides, he called two days ago, he said the money would be even more than he expected. Lots more—we'd be able to renovate. He was wild for that. New modern-type shelves, better lighting, a decent floor."

Celia looked out at the lobby. Down there, two nights ago, Bernie had told her to visit if she ever came to New York. "Did he tell you where that extra money was coming from?"

"He said a debt from long ago." But for a second, doubtfulness on the scrawny face, as if she's asking herself the obvious questions. A debt for what service? Why come to a small scenic town in Vermont to collect it? Why should the process of collecting have gone on for a week?

"They don't understand about Bernie. They think it's

me. Me expecting him to keep some silly promise. It's the store; I know perfectly well that's what he loves. Sometimes he stays till ten o'clock, just fiddling, little changes here and there. If ever he's sick, he can't stand it. He calls in every hour. How are we doing? How many customers? What about that order for long-haired brushes?" She raised her sad, candid, ugly face: See, I know my limitations.

"That's why I came up here. I was desperate. When I called the Inn they said yes, he'd been here, he was with those people."

Those people. Celia came down a step. "How about his family?"

"He has no family. No friends either, if it comes to that. Just me." It was her old apologetic voice. She had shifted again, the anger displaced, as if the basic dubiety had added its inexorable weight to Marcia's and Jill's forthright opinions.

Celia stood next to her. "I bet you're starved. The dining room's closed, but there's a nice place just the other side of the green. I'd be glad to—"

But Janet was shaking her head. She wasn't hungry. She'd just drive back now. She could see it was no use.

"You're going to start right away? That long drive, no rest at all?"

"I don't mind. Maybe when I get home, he'll be there." But she knew Bernie, always on the button, she didn't believe it for a second.

Celia watched her, the navy dress an anomalous dark spot, as Bernie's suit had been, among the plaids and sweaters in the lobby. Then she went upstairs where the phone was already ringing. "Celia? Everything all right?"

All right?—not exactly; with an effort, she wrenched her mind back to this morning. She told it briefly. The fire. The injuries. The hospital. And at Professor Ellsworth's house, the change of guard. "He feels terrible about the fire, of course—Lester, his ailing father, all that. But as for having Madeleine and Jerry there, he doesn't mind, in fact he sort of likes it. A shift in the dull routine—wait, you can hear the tape."

She sat back as it played: "One's own family taking care, attuned to the special wishes, geared for the extra indulgences, prepared to give the unaccustomed treats—it does set one up. And of course a new set of discerning ears—what every teacher once in a while needs for inspiration. . . ."

It doesn't bother her so much this time. Or, rather, it bothers her differently. Rejection, that weak-kneed, submissive feeling? Nonsense. What stirs inside her is simple outrage; like Janet in that brief moment on the stairs, she's gone from self-pity to anger. Really, the idea of his talking like that with her sitting there, a man of intelligence, sensibility. Even if he meant it, it was tactless of him to say it; it shows that under that beautiful lined face, the eloquent voice, there's nothing but an old man's egoism. Elderly self-centeredness. Just because he says he's selfish doesn't excuse it, in fact makes it worse.

She stared out the window as the tape went on. Lucky visitors, enjoying the soft night air, the twisting path through the green, the sparkle of that pretty gazebo.

"No wonder in the end she chooses Mrs. Wix. What she wants is for Maisie to be happy, Maisie's happiness is indeed her sole aim."

A pause after she clicked it off. She could hear Jason clear his throat. What's he going to say? Very interesting? Funny what he said about a new set of discerning ears? He's an old man, Celia, be indulgent?

She gave him no chance to say anything. "Listen. I've had it with this job. I just took it so I could find out about George's death, but there's no way I'm going to find out, by now I don't even give a damn. He's dead and that's that.

I mean, it was a dumb idea for me to come in the first place, well, you always thought that, didn't you?"

Not at all the way she'd planned. Sitting in the dining room where she had made her decision, she'd envisioned her offhand voice, her coolly dismissive words: Celia Sommerville, above it all. Only here she is sounding involved, irritable, defensive, hurt.

"So get someone else. Jason? You there? There must be plenty of candidates. What did Ellsworth specify in that letter? Someone bright and talented? You must know dozens of them." Obviously he does. Those graduate groupies, standing in lovesick hopefulness outside his door. "They'd like it. Good working conditions, you can tell them. This very agreeable Inn, and some breathtaking scenery, and only a couple of hours of real work every day—Jason, you know how to build it up."

"Celia? . . ."

"Oh, and something else. Bernie went off the screen. He owns a hardware and paint store, he and this woman, but he never turned up. He told me what time the bus was getting in and he told the woman what time he'd be there. An important time; with his ill-gotten gains he was going to buy some extra space next door. Or maybe he wasn't, he was looking for a chance to cut loose. How do I know all this? The woman came up. Trip of desperation. No help from Marcia and Jill, who are full of snide suggestions about what a man does when he's hooked up with an unattractive woman and sees a chance to ditch her. So that will be something else for your candidate to look into. Missing person. Add to the fun."

"Celia, look here—"

"Ellsworth's new helper, him or her, think you can get them here by tomorrow? Tomorrow afternoon? Well, the next day latest. I'll sit down with them, play all the tapes, sort of ease them in. And good working conditions, you can promise them that, this nice hotel—well, I said that, didn't I? Anyhow, you'd better get on with it. I'll go for one more day and that's it."

But she did not go for one more day. Because when she got there the next morning, Madeleine Ellsworth told her the professor could not see her.

16

"NO DICTATION TODAY," Madeleine said, and whisked at the apron she was wearing over her slacks.

"I don't understand." Her usual time—nine-thirty—and Celia stood in the doorway, or rather in front of it. Madeleine's figure occupied whatever portion of the doorway she'd left accessible.

"Nothing to understand. He's not feeling well."

"Did you have a doctor?"

"Celia, I think you can leave to us the question of whether or not a doctor is needed."

Bingo. She's done it again. Put me in my place. "I just want to tell him something. Take me a minute."

"Tell me and I'll pass on the message," Madeleine said, anyone might have guessed she would say.

For a second Celia thought about pushing past. She might be small, but she was wiry and also a good ten years younger; with a surprise surge no reason she couldn't make it past the broad shoulders and trimly rounded hips. Then she saw that Jerry was at the foot of the stairs. Jerry holding a tray but also with a vigilant look on his sallow face. Besides, supposing she did get up there, what would she say, how would she conduct herself? Celia, the protection squad. The wild thought went through her mind that it was all her fault: fate punishing her for her ungracious thoughts about Professor Ellsworth last night.

"How about this afternoon?" she asked. "I usually come again at two."

Madeleine nodded, to indicate that she was aware when Celia usually came, but all she said was in her opinion it would be wiser to wait till tomorrow. Or even the next day. Though Celia was of course at liberty to try whenever she liked.

She felt the blast of helplessness. She'd been perfectly sincere last night telling Jason she wanted to quit working for Professor Ellsworth, and now she was sincere in the overwhelming desire to sit in that breezy room, hear the mild greeting from the figure under the plaid blanket, feel the expectant pause before she turned on the machine. The old syndrome: we don't want it till we can't have it.

Well, she was not going to accomplish anything by standing here. Besides, it was raining, a thin rain that fell on her but not on Madeleine, which made her position even more untenable. But as she turned, she saw that a man was coming up the path. "Good morning." He had the resonant voice of a professional speaker, and a smile of professional calm, and he said he was the Reverend Matthews, minister of the First Congregational Church in Anchorville.

"How do you do."

"I'm here to see Professor Ellsworth. Are you by any chance related to him?"

"I'm his daughter-in-law, and this is Miss Sommerville, who works for him."

"A pleasure to meet you both." But the tactical smile was now aimed at Madeleine. "I have an appointment with your father-in-law for ten-thirty. I know I'm early, but since I was in the neighborhood, I thought perhaps . . ."

"He didn't tell me about any appointment."

"I understand he doesn't talk on the phone. But the man

who takes care of him—is his name Lester?—he told me the professor wanted to see me."

The rain was heavier; Madeleine looked sideways as drops fell noisily on a small watering can beside the door. "I'm afraid you were got here on false pretenses, Reverend. I know my father-in-law; you'll forgive me if I say the last thing he's interested in is anything connected with religion."

"I see." More professionalism in his ability to receive with equanimity the unqualified bluntness of that statement. "Perhaps, then, I might speak to Lester so we can check this out."

"Lester's not here. There was a fire at his home night before last."

"Ah. He's the one. I didn't make the connection."

Madeleine put a lightly inquiring hand to her hair. "Lester's a good nurse, but he sometimes takes matters into his own hands. He seems to think that an old man, a rather sick old man—okay, Reverend, I'll come out and say it. Because Lester goes to church himself, he thinks he knows what Professor Ellsworth needs better than the professor does himself. But religion isn't something one person can impose on another, or don't you agree?"

Oh, he did, he surely did.

"I'm sorry you had to come for nothing. And now if you'll excuse me." She didn't bang the door but a definitive closing nonetheless, one that left Celia and the man standing outside in the rain.

"So. I got my walking papers," Mr. Matthews said.

"I didn't do so well either," Celia murmured, but though the man nodded, she had the feeling he wasn't listening, he was working on some problem of his own.

"Funny," he said, as they stepped over puddles in the flagstone walk. "The way that fellow Lester put it, I got the idea it wasn't religion at all Professor Ellsworth wanted to talk about. Unless I badly misunderstood, or of course Lester was trying to mislead me."

Lester would never mislead anyone. She walked on silently.

"My impression was simply that Ellsworth felt a need to talk to someone—a moral question, perhaps—and he thought a minister would be appropriate." Again that puzzled hesitation—was he wondering whether to press his case, tackle the intransigent daughter-in-law again? The rain was coming down harder, it fell on his bare head and nice tweed jacket. And also on a face where the practiced serenity had briefly unraveled. "Miss Sommerville, can I offer you a lift?" he finally said.

She said that was her car over in the driveway, and she ran to get to it, though not fast enough; a new cloudburst caught her; her wet blouse stuck to the back of her seat and she felt water squish under her toes as she pressed down on the gas. And still raining when she got to her destination, which was a phone booth at the corner of Main and Warren. The door wouldn't shut properly; with one hand she fumbled in her purse for coins while with the other she wiped moisture from her eyes so she could see to dial.

"Jason? Celia. Just thought you'd want to know. They wouldn't let me in this morning. They say he's sick, but I don't believe it, God no. Not for a second. And I know you think I'm hysterical, I guess I am. You'd be too if you had to stand there while she—" A man encased in a yellow slicker looked up as he passed; talking too loud. "Oh, well, forget it, probably nothing. You think it's nothing anyhow, so make believe I never called."

"Celia, where are you? Wait—"

"Can't wait. I forgot my umbrella and my shoes are soaked and . . . well, I thought I'd mention it, but now I have to run."

Run across the street to the Municipal Building, where

she calmed down. One outburst a morning is enough. She made herself stop at Victory's to examine the pile of sweaters that were on sale, and on the stairs she took out her lipstick and combed through her limp hair, so she was presentable when she stood in front of the sergeant and asked was Officer Hurley in.

Yes. In and friendly and attentive as usual. "Miss Sommerville, can I get you a towel?"

All right, not so presentable. She shook her head and sat in the proffered chair and in a voice that was less overwrought than the one for Jason she told it again. Madeleine Ellsworth and Jerry taking care of the professor.

Hurley nodded. "Good of you to come, Miss Sommerville, but I'm aware of that already. Mrs. Ellsworth phoned me first thing."

I might have known. "Very clever of her."

Another undemonstrative nod: as they'd agreed before, she was surely a clever woman.

"And this morning they wouldn't let me in at all. They said the professor was too sick to work."

"I'm sorry to hear that."

"It doesn't bother you? That she's obviously—oh, don't answer that." She stood and looked out on the parking lot. "I was wondering about that fire," she said.

"Terrible," Hurley said. "That poor man having to suffer. To say nothing of one of the authentic old barns gone."

"Do you know what—I mean, why would a fire start in the middle of the night?"

"Lots of reasons. Someone throws a cigarette. Something's been smoldering. A short circuit in old wires."

"Or arson?"

A quick look from the square face, but still no expression in his voice. Arson was certainly not to be discounted. But he'd known Lester and his brother Arnie for a long time. Even though it was no secret that upkeep was a drain,

164

they'd been interested in getting some money out of the property, he considered it highly unlikely that—

"I wasn't thinking of Lester and Arnie."

Hurley refused to rise to the bait. They were investigating, of course, was all he said.

"The way you're investigating George Theroux's death," she said, and then was sorry.

But the drawling voice was equable. "Miss Sommerville, why don't you say what you have on your mind?"

Once years ago she had walked out on a plank while all around the ice was cracking. She remembered the feeling: awe at her own temerity, panic at the possibility of disaster, envy of those placid onlookers who refused to have anything to do with the exploit. "Suppose Madeleine Ellsworth and Jerry were looking for a way to get the professor alone. Really alone. I mean, they had to get Lester out of the way."

Hurley leaned forward across the desk. "Why would they want that?"

"Oh, my God, isn't it obvious? He's a sick man. Sick, old, feeble. Also, I assume, though it's never mentioned in front of me, on a careful regimen of pills and stuff. So someone on the spot, they'd be in position to withhold a certain medicine, or maybe give an extra dose. . . ."

"Are you suggesting they plan to kill him?"

Still breathless. All this maneuvering and indirection to get to this simple statement. "It wouldn't be the first time a family wanted to kill an old man so they could get his money."

Hurley pushed a pile of papers from one side of the desk to the other. "Miss Sommerville, I thought you understood. They're getting his money. Except for some minor bequests, his will names his family as the recipients of his considerable fortune. He's told me that, I have every reason to believe he's told them."

"Maybe they don't want to wait."

"They don't have to wait very long. We're talking about a man with two years to live. Two at the outside. I'm not sure which of his several ailments is the operative one, but that's the prognosis. Unimpeachable. He knows it, we know it, they know it."

She could hear Lester: If I work for two years, he'll see that we have enough to open a restaurant.

Hurley was still talking. "Miss Sommerville, when you came with the suggestion that the Ellsworths killed your friend George Theroux, I could appreciate it. I didn't agree, but I understood your reasoning. But Professor Ellsworth! His family kill him! If they try anything like it, they stand to lose everything. Don't you see—if you kill someone, you don't inherit their money. That being so, it would be the height of stupidity for them to do any plotting against him. And we just agreed, didn't we, that Madeleine Ellsworth isn't stupid."

Celia was back at the window. So she's done it again, that woman. Faked me out. Put me in my place. Celia Sommerville, made to look foolhardy, ludicrous, blundering, unreasonable.

Hurley was nice; he didn't push it. "Believe me, Miss Sommerville, we take good care of him. We like him. Not just because he's the richest one around. Not even because if anyone on the force gets in a jam, sick child, wife needing an operation, anything like that, quick as a shot Ellsworth is in there with the dough. But something else. The Cedar Springs Police Department has a special feeling for him. Always did have. From long ago, when they'd come in winter, he and his wife and the young boy."

She turned. "You remember that?"

"Now wait a minute. I'm not as old as all that. But my predecessor told me."

"Told you what?"

He paused, hands together: a man making a decision.

166

"Back in those days, when they used to stop a speeding car, it would be the wife driving. Suzanne, that was her name. Only the man next to her, it wouldn't be the professor. Nine times out of ten, not the professor. Well, so policemen are more human than you think. They see a set-up like that, they feel protective. About the husband, that is. Especially in a town like this, lots of stiff New England morality around. No one has to say anything, it just happens. That nice quiet man whose wife is two-timing him, he's someone they look out for. Human nature." Officer Hurley, the small-town philosopher again.

"How about when she died? Suzanne."

"Way I heard it, that happened to be a day the speeding car wasn't spotted. Which was a shame because it went over that cliff on the road past Anchorville. Only that day—it was a night, actually—she was in the car alone. Maybe on her way to a date. Maybe coming back. Or who can tell, maybe a restless woman just out for a spin. I don't know why I'm telling you all this. Yes, Miss Sommerville, I do know," he said in his unhurried country voice. "So you'll let go. Understand that if anyone has to keep an eye on Professor Ellsworth, we're the ones on the job. Time for anyone else to bow out."

17

BOW OUT: HURLEY. Lie low: Jason. All these stark, un-equivocal two-syllabled admonitions to set her on the right course. And in fact she's already told Jason that bowing out is exactly what she is dying to do, what she is going to do as soon as that replacement she has asked for is at hand.

But events have changed, or at least speeded up, since that acrimonious phone conversation last night, and she has thought of an errand that, though it's not exactly bowing in, Hurley with his purist ideas might nevertheless not characterize as bowing out. She leaned her head on the wheel and remembered Les's words: Follow the signs to the horse farm, then left about a mile to the covered bridge—you haven't seen it yet, you'll love it—then right to Brookdale and keep straight: directions to Cedar Springs Preparatory School.

At least no Jerry to spy on her this time: Jerry was carrying trays in the professor's house, where he had decidedly bowed in.

Her windshield wiper inexplicably stopped when she'd gone about a mile, but the rain stopped too, only a faint mist by the time she drove through the gate posts and got out of the car. And no need to look in at the office: a visitor who knew where she was headed, she went confidently along the muddy paths. In front of the place where he used to live—that pretty little place with red shutters that had been preempted for an infirmary—someone had left a poster against the door. BLUE TEAM BASEBALL it said, or once said—the paint ran in speckled streams down the curling front of the cardboard. At the house where he did live, there was no bell, and when she knocked on the door, nothing happened except that a cat dozing under some bushes ran off into the woods behind. Why didn't she call first, as she had last time? PROCEED AT YOUR OWN RISK: the sign still there. Proceed where? Must she walk up the three flights to those quarters that were inadequate to receive visitors?

"Mr. Druer! Mr. Druer!" Her voice cut through the wet silence; she half expected to see animals stick inquiring heads out of the grove of pine trees. But after four or five shouts a window opened. "Why, it's Miss Sommerville. Come on in and I'll be down."

The same lumbering progress down, the same invitation into the large room that once served for picnics or square dances and now by its vaultlike emptiness comprised a statement about the low esteem in which this building was held. But a gratified look on his face as he arranged his cane next to him on the bench and said what could he do for her.

"I was just thinking about the school. The way it used to be, I mean, when your father ran it. I have a friend who has a daughter, fifteen years old and sort of trouble. If she could find a place like that today."

He leaned forward on his elbows. "Don't bother looking. There is no place like that today. No one would run it. No one would come to it. Freedom. Natural fulfillment. Inner happiness. Who wants to hear about that lot?" The bleary eyes focused on her for a dispirited look. "I was going through my father's book the other day. I remember when it was published. What reviews! Stimulating, exciting, challenging, vision, courage . . . what didn't those great educators say? And the preface by a world-famous psychiatrist.

I remember his big statement. There are no problem children. There are only problem parents. Problem humanity. . . . Should I tell you something? A month after the book was published, my father had a great stroke of luck. He died. Just keeled over one morning, age seventy-eight. Best thing that could have happened. He never knew that a year after his beloved book came out, it was out of date. A curiosity—can you tie that! Something for graduate students to write theses about. Times had changed. Different values. His were stimulating, exciting, challenging, maybe, but no one in his right mind would be caught using them."

The cane fell, he waited for Celia to pick it up. "One year when I was still teaching, I showed the book to a couple of friends here at Cedar Springs. I remember two lines that really got them. 'Most of the school work that adolescents do is simply a waste of time and energy and patience. It robs youth of its right to play and play and play; it puts old heads on young shoulders.' What a laugh they got out of that. Play and play and play. How were those young dunderheads going to pull up their SATs with that system? Where would you find parents to write out the checks for tuition?"

His voice cracked with the weight of his agitated sincerity, and for a second she felt guilty. She's exploiting him, egging him on. All these emotions activated, just so she can subtly work the conversation around to Roy Ellsworth.

"One day last month someone drove me to the lake where my father sometimes took us. Great spot, about an hour from here. We used to go swimming naked. All of us. Boys, girls, men, women. If you don't make a fuss, there'll be no undue interest, my father used to say. Thank the good lord he doesn't have to see that lake today. They're naked too now, or almost naked, but what a difference. I can just hear him. He'd stand on that strip of rocky beach and look at the suits that are just a string here, a string there, and he'd say, That kind of nakedness thinks there's something dirty about sex, it calls you to leer at it, it's sick, sick, sick."

A great sigh from the hunched over shoulders. "Opinionated, my old man, he'd be the first to admit. But he got results; you have to hand it to him. The boys learned. All that sitting under trees, but when push came to shove, the boys really did learn. A miracle: those that wanted passed exams. And there was less snickering. Less nastiness. You didn't have to go around with a flashlight to see who was sneaking off to the woods to do what they couldn't do in their dorm room."

A sudden surge of noise outside, laughter, shouts—Come on, you guys. The Blue Team back in business, now the rain has stopped? "How about the years when you were a teacher? Much sneaking off in the woods then?"

She was briefly the object of the lidded gaze. "You want to know about young Ellsworth, don't you?"

So: not as subtle as I thought. "Okay, I do want. Anything about him and his roommate George."

"Not just idle curiosity, I hope." Momentarily, a teacher's voice, with the right to question, severely probe.

"Oh, Mr. Druer, believe me. George committed suicide is what they say, but I don't think—"

"That's all right." Back with memory again. "Not George," he said then. "That uptight boy, he'd do everything right. Would he ever break a rule? Not him. Too good an opinion of himself. Too careful. It was Roy."

The screams outside were louder. Hey, Toby. Wait up for Toby, you guys. "What kind of rule did Roy Ellsworth break, Mr. Druer?"

Old people, how brief their span of concentration. One minute, that close attention, the next subsiding into the dreamy abstractions. In a second he'd be back with role confusion, ego identity. "Mr. Druer, what about Roy?"

The watery eyes looked up, focusing on the beams that

171

crisscrossed the ceiling. "Didn't get on with his father. Wouldn't see him."

Mr. Druer, I know, I know.

"Kid like Roy, trouble in one area, you look for trouble in another. There was a cousin," he said. "Tall skinny kid. Blond, let's see . . ."

"Lee," she said. "Lee Elliott."

"Sure enough, that was his name." He accepted it without surprise, letting his elbows slide further along the table. "He visited on one of those vacations when Roy wouldn't go home. Stayed in his dorm room. Strictly forbidden. Someone who's not enrolled at the school living in a room that—Miss Sommerville, you okay?"

"Yes." No. God, no. I banked everything on just the opposite: finding her out in a lie, pinning her down with her own clever deceptions. Why else did I come here, encourage that long-winded introduction? Only now her story turns out to be correct, confirmed by this disinterested observer with his wandering attention, his erratic memories.

"Who was it found them that time in the woods? Old Havermill, Latin teacher? No, his family lived down south, he never stayed around on vacations. Lyons, math? Not him either. I know. It was Jodie, the janitor—can you tie that! Busybody, that one, wanted to curry favor, figured if he told—"

"Told what?"

"What they were doing. You know."

She sat silent. Damn, damn.

"Not so nice. Not even local girls, those pretty waitresses, say—that would be bad enough. These were friends of that cousin; he actually brought them. Imported, you might say."

"Girls?"

The rambling tone sharpened. "Sure enough, girls. What did you expect two sixteen-year-old boys to have out there under the pines?"

172

"I thought maybe you were going to say—well, cousins. Close. Fond of each other . . ."

"You mean gay? They do call it gay now, don't they? Funny word. 'Queer' in my day, just as bad. Oh, I can understand your mistake, but not Roy. Never Roy. A good thing too. That business with his father, he had enough headaches without that."

"I thought maybe that was the problem with the father." She spoke slowly, full weight to every word. "I mean, the father sort of guessed, and he objected, or anyhow made nasty remarks about it . . . Well, all the inevitable strain."

"I wish Jodie was here. That fellow who found them in the woods. He'd set you straight soon enough."

"Ah."

"Besides, that roommate of his. George. Didn't I tell you how uptight? Whatever he knew about Roy, if he did know anything, it wasn't that. Gay—that wasn't the kind of thing George Theroux would put up with in someone he lived with for three years."

"Mr. Druer, are you sure?"

He was again focused on the distant ceiling, that gaze that was an auxiliary to his focusing on the distant past. "Oh, my dear. They can keep it from friends, from parents, from someone they mow lawns for over the summer, but from the staff at their prep school? Never, never. When I was very young"—leaning forward now, the voice of strained sincerity—"my father sent me to a school where they watched our bowels. Did we perform every day?—someone always knew. Don't ask me how, just there it was. Before bedtime they'd point to the boys who were to come up for their dose of laxative. You, You, You, and that one there in the blue shirt—You! Same way with us here at Cedar Springs. Their sexual proclivities, that was our business. More important than their grades in French, their standing on the tennis team. Was Roy Ellsworth gay—Miss Sommerville, not a chance."

"Mr. Druer, thank you." Thank you more than I can say. Because now it's definite. She lied to me. All that saga— Roy and his cousin starting their affair during a prep school vacation; Roy and his rigid, intolerant father; Roy handing out generous sums to Lee Elliott because this man's life had been ruined; and of course George: George ready to betray his old friend, give the disheartening news to Roy's children unless the payments were made—lies, lies. All that pathos and courage and heartbreak, doled out by a woman down by the brook—all a skillful and persuasive lie.

Stepping into a puddle on the way out, Celia laughed; she aimed a smile at the bedraggled members of the Blue Team carrying bats and gloves down the road; she sent a jovial wave to the surprised man wiping his shoes in front of the office—carrying her treasure, which was the incontestable proof of Madeleine Ellsworth's duplicity. She felt light, weightless.

But when she slid her damp body under the wheel, realization set in. What's she going to do with this treasure, this gift she's got by her own resourcefulness? Share it with Officer Hurley? Sit opposite that square undemonstrative face that pretends to be impartial but is really linked by bonds of long standing to the Ellsworth family? Bow out, Miss Sommerville. Trust us. We're investigating. Bow out.

Besides, what is this great treasure she's carrying except something negative? At least, what would Hurley say it was except something negative? "So Madeleine Ellsworth fed you a line, Miss Sommerville; why should that be so important?" "But don't you see, she just did it so I'd stop probing into their affairs." "Well, of course no one really is comfortable with a stranger probing into their affairs." "Oh, it's not that, believe me, there's some evidence she doesn't want me to find." "And have you any idea, Miss Sommerville, what that evidence might be?" "I wish to God I did, I mean, it's there, I know . . . if only . . ."

In the end she drove back to the house. No, not all the

way back. Something—prudence? fear?—made her park a block away, then she walked along the road till she came to the line of shrubbery that separated the Ellsworth property from the more carefully trimmed lawn next door. A doctor's lawn; every day she admires the yellow sign that hangs like a flag over his gate. What kind of doctor? Internist? Pediatrician? Or, this town where skiing is the cottage industry, does he make an easy living setting bones broken on the ski slopes? In any case, surely he won't mind if she walks on his lawn so she can slide between the bushes at just the point where she is parallel with the professor's front door.

But when she got there, in that tangle of wet branches and brown stems and dried pods, she saw it was no use. Only the caw of a crow, the bark of a distant dog to disturb the heavy country stillness, but still from her position here she couldn't hear what was going on in that large breezy front room upstairs. He could be calling for help, saying, Get someone, Get the police, and she would not hear.

Besides, why should he call for help, what's to provoke it. If you kill someone you don't inherit: Officer Hurley. Crouching slightly to keep the twigs and leaves out of her face, she moved forward, along the moist encumbered ground, till she was opposite the window of Roy's room she had looked out of yesterday. Nothing untoward about the place now, as there had been nothing when she was up there. Not even any car parked here today; all that was visible were the three steps between house and driveway and the mass of neglected lilies in what must once have been a splendid bed. So why did Madeleine go into such a turmoil? A woman whose steely control provides her with a dignified demeanor on all occasions. When that impudent Cindy says something wrong at table, when it's necessary that Celia be subtly discomfited, when the subject of suicide is up for validation, when she is telling a story of which every false detail has been worked out to perfectly accommodate every troublesome fact—at all these times, there she is, holding herself in, training her words to conform to the chosen pattern. So what was there about the presence of Celia at that window that threw her, wrenched her out of her masterful serenity? "Move your ass away from that window": shrew for an instant.

Celia looked sideways. The lilies are not the only objects of neglect. She can see a few chrysanthemums trying to find themselves breathing space, a delphinium almost flat along the ground, some slimy stalks of bleeding heart—how mistaken they are, these persistent perennials, thinking it's still the era of Suzanne: the era when, as Mattie Haines said, there was a crew of servants at each of the vacation houses, ready at a moment's notice to serve a meal and bring in the iced drinks. Now no one even bothers to pull the weeds that squirm out between the stones on the front walk where she and the Reverend Matthews were dismissed this morning.

Another question: what was that man doing here? Madeleine said it was because Lester was imbued with the kind of missionary zeal that would push faith on Professor Ellsworth whether he asked for it or not, and Mr. Matthews said he had got the idea that the professor simply wanted to talk to him about some moral question. So which?

Well, to be honest, she can imagine Lester prepared to acquire for his employer the blessings of religion. There's a strain of naiveté about him, a simple goodness; in getting a minister to pay a surprise visit, he would not think he was showing presumption but offering salvation. You can't take care of someone whose days are numbered without having that fact as a constant in your thoughts; if Lester truly gets a lift from some religious practice himself, only natural that he would want to pass on this benefit to someone even more needful.

On the other hand—she shifted sideways when a bramble

scratched her arm—it's undeniable that a gratuitous mention of morality in one form or other is a feature of almost every discussion by the professor. "All authors lucky in a sense. In position, as we humans are not, to dole out whatever punishments they think are due. And then live comfortably with themselves in the conviction that justice has been done." Ellsworth taking off from *The Mill on the Floss.* "Children, what makes them act the way they do? How much can you blame on parents, how much can parents blame on the mandates of their time?" Ellsworth, on his first dictation to her. "However they turn out, best to remember you have a part in it." Ellsworth explaining to Hurley why he acquiesces in all the considerable failings of his family. In fact, now she thinks of it, what's his whole book but an attempt to rationalize for himself the fact that a man of his stature has ended up with such a crummy bunch of grandchildren?

Or is he wrestling with more than just the fact of disappointing grandchildren, is there a troubled soul behind the creamy rhetoric? She looked toward the windows of that front room; still quiet up there, the only sound is distant thunder. But though the rain keeps holding off, the air here in her green shingled house is heavy. Entombed by dampness, by overgrown branches, by moisture from the earth itself, she feels unable to breathe. If only someone would walk up. The postman. A milk truck. A boy on a bicycle bringing the meat for tonight's supper. Or maybe Lester, come to report that things with his father are better/not better, and how is everything going around here? When you think of all the people who in the normal course of events have reason to approach the Ellsworth house. She'll take anyone. Any diversion, to stop the words rattling around in her head. If you kill someone, you don't inherit. How much can you blame on parents? The conviction that justice has been done. Remember you have a part in it. In position to dole out the punishment. Move your ass away from that window. If you kill someone, you don't inherit. . . . The words kept sounding, a fugue that drew on past, on present, then back to that indecipherable past again, and with a sudden jolt, so her arm was scratched by some bramble, she realized she had deciphered it, she knew what it was that George knew, the knowledge that sent him to his death.

18

SHE KNOWS, AND it's pure speculation. She has no proof at all. Her theory dovetails with every circumstance and coincides with the characters of those involved, but so did Madeleine's story. Wrong: Madeleine's story dovetailed more forcefully with the facts, coincided more accurately with the characters. All she, Celia, has, when you come down to it, is a guess; one that would offend Hurley's instincts, tax his patronizing good humor, evoke his philosophic disclaimers—and leave the situation exactly where it is, with Madeleine and Jerry in charge of the professor.

As if to mock her, the front door opened, Jerry came out on the steps. Is he preparing to leave? No, he's just going to stand there, his face bored, languid, empty. He'll stand there and she'd better not move. One look and he'll guess what she has just discerned. Or at least he will call his mother; between them they will guess. There's a symbiosis: I've seen into their minds, they'll see into mine. They'll size me up, my damp clothing, my excited face, my furtive position, and it will come over them that I know everything George did, I'm the same menace George was. No, worse than George. He merely desired money; I want justice, retribution, a great outpouring of the facts.

Does she really believe this? Well, one part of her cravenly does, while the other part points out that it's nonsense; there's no way Jerry and Madeleine can guess what she knows. Looking at her will tell them nothing—that's common sense. They think their secret is safe, and unless she's fool enough to say something outright, they'll go on thinking it.

And if she's right, what a secret. Celia and George, the only ones, aside from the principals, to know it. Funny. Five days ago she sat with him at a restaurant and spoke the words to end the relationship, and since then she's been more involved with him than ever before. She can even sympathize with him. Well, no, not sympathize—simply see it as George must have seen it. After all, those many years when he gave his support, his loyalty, his steadfastness, his silence. And then finally that uptightness, as Mr. Druer calls it, snapping. Like one who, at age fifty, takes a first sip of wine and turns into an alcoholic. That virtuous George deciding that it's time for him to get some mileage out of what he knows. Turn it to his favor. And he would not have demanded anything unreasonable—not George. No permanent subsidy. Simply enough so that one who had always lived on an academic salary could buy the house he coveted. He would have balanced it in that methodical mind: the loss of innocence against a pond, an orchard, a splendid example of Gothic Revival architecture. But what he failed to realize was that for those others it would not seem reasonable at all. To them he must have been a man with a time bomb, ready to blow up everything they had worked for.

"Right here." She jumped. A human voice. Only Jerry, she realized. Now where'd you go? Madeleine must have called, and I'm right here, he told her. Right here must bore him silly. Carrying an old man's trays, adjusting his window, helping him in and out of bed, even eating the kind of meals that are mandated for his invalid regimen—how that night character, that car thief, that high liver must hate it.

He'll hate it, but he'll stick it out. For how long? Well, for whatever time is necessary. Until they have accomplished their purpose. Or, rather, made sure no one accomplishes a purpose to undercut their grand design. Meanwhile, up there, an old man sits. Sick perhaps, frail surely, a prisoner beyond doubt. Threatened, thwarted, as a prisoner always is. So maybe the real question is, how long can Professor Ellsworth stick it out? Knowing perfectly well why he is imprisoned, what message is being imparted under the fake helpfulness, how long can his ailing constitution take it?

If she just had something definite. One small bit of evidence to nail them. Or someone simply to appraise her theory, give her a reading on its validity. Someone dispassionate who knows the facts, could weigh them, tell her whether she has something or whether because of frustration and general hysteria she's gone off the deep end. But the only one in this category is Jason, and he's made clear that he's not interested, count him out, he's had it with the Ellsworths. Damn Jason, raising her hopes and then crassly letting her down.

Anyhow, why this sudden focus on Jason? Is it because a voice at the door sounds like him? A voice saying, "I'm his new nurse, he expects me." All this long time in a dark place—maybe she's hallucinating. She pushed aside a branch so she could get a view of the doorway. Two people standing there now: Jerry and a man in a nurse's uniform: stiff white jacket, white pants, white shoes.

"Bill Ford's the name," the voice that sounded like Jason's but could not possibly be his was saying. "Professor Ellsworth asked me to come."

An indistinct growl from Jerry. No visitors. The professor wasn't seeing anyone.

"I'm not a visitor," the pseudo-Jason said. "I'm his new nurse. I'm supposed to start working today."

"There must be some mistake."

"No mistake, I assure you." A step nearer the door by the man who from the back does indeed resemble Jason.

The long lean frame. The bony shoulders. The blondish hair growing untidily on the long neck. Jason and a million others. "The Association was very clear about the job."

"What Association is that?"

Mild indignation in the pseudo-Jason's voice, as if to say, Any damn fool would know. "Association of Trained Male Nurses, Northeast Division."

"What do they have to do with Professor Ellsworth?"

"They filled his order, that's what. Very precise specifications as to age, training, temperament, what not. Not an easy man to satisfy, your Mr. Ellsworth. They tell me the computer went through a hundred names before it landed on me."

"Get lost," Jerry said after a pause.

"When I've just thrown over another job, a perfectly good one, and given up chance of a bonus besides, not very likely."

"Sorry. You can't come in." The growl had turned plaintive, querulous—Madeleine would do better, Celia thought. With brainy Madeleine at the door, things would be different. She would devise something, some drastic and irrefutable response: the man in the white uniform would be summarily dismissed, as Celia was dismissed, as the Reverend Matthews was dismissed. But Jerry was different. All bluster and no brains.

So when the male nurse said, "Look here, if you don't let me in pronto, three of my colleagues who are over at the hospital will be here to see that I get in," when he made that threat, though a little scuffle ensued at the door, a collision of pushing arms and obdurate shoulders, it lasted less than a minute—as she watched, the figure in the white coat went through the door, which then closed behind him.

Now what? She leaned against a tree and closed her eyes, and she was inside that contentious house. The male nurse is crossing the front hall off which the unused living room opens, he has put his white-clad foot on the bottom step,

182

when Madeleine comes out of the kitchen. "Where do you think you're going?" she demands. The male nurse answers courteously without however slowing his progress: He's been hired to work for a Professor Eric Ellsworth of this address. "Who gave you the authority?" Madeleine says, puffing a little because she has to keep up with him on the broad staircase. In the same tone of reproachful surprise he used to Jerry, he repeats the name of his Association. "Show me your papers," she says. "I'm sure the Association will be glad to show them," he answers. "Shall I give you their address?" Madeleine's voice rises, it's closer to the voice with which she said, Move your ass away from that window. "You can't go up without papers, just get out of here." "Excuse me, Madame," he says, "as I explained to your son—it is your son, isn't it?—I was told to be here at noon. Past that already, I'm afraid." "You can't go in, he doesn't want you," she shouts. "We'll put the matter to him and let him decide," the nurse says, and having reached the door of the room, gives the same push to Madeleine's prohibiting shoulders that was so effective with Jerry outside. "I tried to tell him—" Jerry begins, from his position two or three feet behind, but his mother isn't having any. "Idiot!" she mutters. She starts to follow the nurse, but stops, the man is alone when he enters the professor's room and says—

What does he say? How does Ellsworth answer? Maybe if she knew the identity of that figure in the white jacket, she could go on with this vivid scenario—as is, her powers of invention are used up. At least she doesn't have to stay hidden any longer, trapped between wet branches. She can come out on the lawn. If the nurse happens to look out the front window—Little too much breeze in here, Professor Ellsworth may say—he may invite her in, especially as it's once more starting to rain. But though she stood in full view of that critical window, no invitation ensued.

No invitation, nothing for her to do but wait. Wait for

how long? She doesn't even know what time it is. On a bright day, she can guess the hour by the shadow of the tree beside the front door—the steps are in full shade when she comes for the afternoon session. But no clues now, no hint of what's ahead.

What's she doing here anyhow, where nothing happens as you expect it? She has no experience with this kind of agenda; the essence of her life is planning. Sitting at her desk in June, she makes the arrangements to ensure that the inauguration of the new college president in November will go off as intended. Food, flowers, speakers, halls: every detail covered, every contingency foreseen. And after that event, another and then another; an institutional year in which Celia Sommerville's role is to see that the unexpected does not happen, there is no room for it.

Besides, she's unused to solitude. Making these arrangements entails talking, sometimes constant talking, sometimes talking so interminable a protective secretary takes measures to curtail it. Sorry, Miss Sommerville has just stepped out. No, I'm afraid Miss Sommerville can't speak to you just now. Once in a while she thinks, Lucky people who don't have to talk at their work, if I could just have that, a day without phone calls, conferences, interviews, meetings. She will never think it again. Maybe the bag ladies, those women who sit muttering obscurely on park benches, feel like this: a great longing for contact, any contact. Right this minute, the most inane remark would fill the bill. Why doesn't it rain hard and get it over with? Maybe the grass is happy. Good weather for ducks.

But when someone did come, still no chance of communication. It was an ambulance, CEDAR SPRINGS—ANCHORVILLE HOSPITAL CENTER in the requisite red letters on its white sides, and the two men who hopped out walked past without a glance at either side. Chins set, shoulders swinging, hands firm on the stretcher rolled up between them: men trained at coming to the rescue.

184

Rescue for whom? The professor, of course. No one had to commit murder. Simply the realization that he was a prisoner, that they intended to keep him a prisoner—this put the final strain on a weakened heart. They'll try everything, those experienced medics, but it will be too late. Dead on arrival, hospital records will show.

Or maybe the one they have to rescue is that nurse. Yes, that's it; she sees it now. Jerry and Madeleine assaulted that white-clad figure just as he was about to walk into Professor Ellsworth's room. That's why she couldn't picture the scene before: too ugly. He got almost to the door, this intruder who might be capable of messing everything up, and Jerry took the heavy chair that stands in the hall and brought it down, smash, on the man's head. A concussion? Yes, a bad one, he lies unconscious while Madeleine with her masterful persuasion explains to the medics how he broke in, he uttered threats, he was violent, they had no recourse except to disarm him.

But if that is true, why is Jason walking out now behind the stretcher. Or at least the man she thought resembled Jason and who looks even more like him now she can see him full face. She would know for sure if when he turned to her there would be a glimmer of recognition. A wink, an infinitesimal wave, a lift of eyebrow. There is nothing. He looks at her, through her, as though she is part of the scenery, of no more consequence than the gate post, the plum tree with its sagging branches, the bed of straggling lilies. His gaze rakes in all that, and then he gives his attention to the man on the stretcher. Him she can recognize, though only the top half of his head emerges from the blanket. It is Professor Ellsworth, and though his eyes are closed he must be alive because the man who may or may not be Jason is patting his hand.

Jerry and Madeleine ignored her too, or at least pointedly refrained from looking at the spot where she was standing. That was different. They themselves were being ignored.

They were behind the procession but not part of it; they walked with the defiant swagger of people who have been excluded and want to show how little it matters; when the stretcher arrived at the back door of the ambulance, they remained a few feet distant while the medics and the nurse talked. A brief conference, then the stretcher with trained delicacy was lifted inside.

But they didn't drive right off. One of the medics, that implacable nurse, the Ellsworths at their enforced distance, she herself—all stood, an unlikely tableau on the damp lawn. Why the delay? Don't ambulances always move at top speed? Even if there is no emergency, isn't speed, complete with siren sounding, red light flashing, part of the accepted ritual? Then a car drove up, and she understood.

She'd seen Officer Hurley only behind a desk. Now, getting out of a car, he seemed larger. There was an aggressive tilt, an urgency that was lacking when he sat down—more the policeman than the philosopher. But he stood for a calmly deliberate talk with the nurse and the medic, then he waited till the ambulance drove off before he went over to Madeleine and Jerry. "Back to the hotel"—is that what he told those two excluded characters? Possibly, because when he came over to her, his message was the same. "You go on back to the hotel, Miss Sommerville. I'll be along when I can."

19

GO ON BACK TO the hotel: another admonition from Hurley. Well, she's at the hotel, she's been here for eight hours. Eight hours of walking back and forth on the porch, going up to her room and coming precipitously down, holding a magazine unread, leaning over the railing at each sound of a car driving up.

She's not the only one. Though at various times she saw one or another Ellsworth go into the dining room, in each case it was an aborted meal. Ten minutes later there they would be again, tight lipped, stiff legged, silent on the porch. And always different combinations. Jill and Madeleine. Cindy and Jerry. Jerry and Marcia. People restless but alert, keeping an eye on each other and also, maybe, on Celia Sommerville. Or one of them would go over to the phone booth, where presumably they got from the hospital the same message she did: Professor Ellsworth's condition is stable. Stable: a word invented by bureaucracy, designed to convey nothing.

All of them except Jill were on the porch when the nurse who called himself Bill Ford came at last. She knew he had come before he appeared on the steps: the stiffening of Jerry's back, the meaningful nod to his mother, the creak of Marcia's chair as it tilted abruptly forward. Well, she can't blame them. She feels stiff too. Stiff, apprehensive, puzzled.

Will he acknowledge her now, this man whose arrival has changed everything? Will he come out with explanations? Will his presence provide a consummation of sorts?

The entrance lights shone directly on his face when he came up on the porch, and she thought, Jason, of course. And he saw her, there was no doubt that his gaze took her in. But it was to Jerry he went. Jerry, Madeleine, Marcia, and a second later Cindy and Jill.

Jerry leaned against the railing. "So how is he? My grandfather."

Jason paused. Was he gearing himself to the hostility implicit in Jerry's speech? Or was he simply waiting till she, Celia, had a chance to walk over and position herself behind them? "Not too bad," he said then. "Not too bad."

"What the hell does that mean?" Jerry's voice sounded thick.

"You know. Pulse steady, blood pressure in the acceptable range, vital signs okay."

"Is he conscious, can he talk, what does he say?"

Another pause. Jason laid a light hand on a geranium, standing pink and dewy in the artificial light. "What does a man in a hospital say? Raise me up. Let me down. I'm thirsty. How long do I have to stay here? Crusty old gentleman, your grandfather."

"So how long must he stay?" Marcia, speaking up.

"Well, they're doing tests, this and that. You know hospitals once they get hold of you." Then his quizzical glance rested on Madeleine. "Ma'am, are all these nice people your family?"

"Oh. I forgot. My daughters." One by one, she named them. Marcia. Gillian. Cindy. Then a grudging pause, and she went on. "And this is Celia Sommerville. She's working for Professor Ellsworth this summer."

Jason—oh God, despite the white uniform and the blank stare it is Jason, isn't it?—said he was pleased to meet them all.

"You're his nurse?" Cindy asked.

"His day nurse. He has a night nurse on duty now."

"I never saw a man nurse before." Cindy's mouth was set in a pout, as if to say, if she hadn't seen one, they couldn't be so great.

"There are lots of us," Jason said brightly. "Very important branch of the profession."

"Don't you mind?"

"Mind?" His face retained the impersonal smile.

"Doing woman's work." The pout turned into a little smirk: the Cindy trademark.

Jason's gaze went around to all of them. "I guess this young lady needs some indoctrination in the subject of gender roles."

No one smiled. No one was in the mood for smiling.

"I mean, suppose it's a woman patient you have to take care of."

As Jason launched into his explanation, when people are sick, it's their condition that counts, turning a patient to avoid bed sores you don't think are they male or female—as his patient voice went over the banal details, Celia thought, What would these tense people do without Cindy? They can look at her with indignation, Cindy the monster, but she talks, she keeps it going, right now she's what saves them.

Then Madeleine made an effort and asked Mr. Ford if he thought the hospital was adequate.

"Call me Bill." He gave his polite male-nurse smile. "The hospital? Actually, I think it's fine. They all know the old gent. Seem to be truly concerned about him. Sometimes that's more important than anything else."

For the first time, his eyes met Celia's. Old gent: How do you like that?

"We could easily have him transported by helicopter to another hospital," Madeleine suggested.

But Jason said he thought Professor Ellsworth was right

189

where he wished to be, and looked out at the view, which tonight consisted of only clouds and mist.

"How about food? He's so particular." Madeleine, still the solicitous daughter-in-law: you had to give her credit.

Jason said he seemed to be satisfied with what they gave him, and then turned; a bellboy had come out and was whispering in his ear. He cleared his throat. Would they excuse him? Phone call for him.

"I hope it's not bad news about the professor."

"They would call *you*, Ma'am," he told Madeleine with a deferential bow.

"This hick town, can't tell what anyone might do," Jerry mumbled.

"Hick town! Watch it, boy," Marcia said and looked along the porch. She didn't have to worry; no one coming over to them. No one would come over, Celia thought. Hotel guests have highly developed instincts; though half a dozen people were standing around who in the normal course of events would stop for a chat, a word about the weather, something about the Ellsworth group sent out a message of unapproachability.

So when Jason came back, they were still in the same tight group at one end of the porch. He wore his helpful smile. Not to worry. The phone call was not about Professor Ellsworth. At least, not about him directly. Simply someone who wants to see him.

"See him?"

"Visit him in the hospital. Fellow said he had something to tell him."

"So why'd he call you?" Madeleine asked.

"He couldn't get through to the room, so the hospital switchboard told him to try me. Small-town hospitals"—he put out his hands: don't blame me, folks—"everyone knows everything."

"Didn't you tell him no visitors?"

"Oh, I did, of course." Jason stood with his back to the

flower boxes. "But he sounded nervy. He said, Don't worry, they can't keep me out. Or something to that effect."

"Maybe you should alert them," Jerry said. "Tell them there's somebody out to make trouble. Did he give his name, this nervy guy?"

"Let's see," the male nurse said. "Lenox, I think it was. Bernie Lenox."

"Bernie! So he's not lost," Cindy squealed. No one paid attention. No one turned to her. When her last word died away, the silence was complete. "Can't be Bernie," Marcia said at last.

Celia saw that Jill was scraping the arm of her wicker chair. Little shreds of green paint were spread around her on the floor.

"I wrote it down," the male nurse said. "I always think that's best when I'm on a case and other people . . . Oh, here." He tilted his head, holding a piece of paper to the light. "B. Lenox, all right. Someone you folks know?"

The silence this time was more portentous. Then Marcia put her hand to her hair. "He left here two days ago. He wouldn't be coming back."

"Why not?" Cindy the monster again. At least, the one they all glare at as if she is some incomprehensible kind of monster. "Bernie getting lost!—I knew that was crazy. He'd never let himself be lost. He'd write down in his note-book where he was every second."

In the air of inattention that followed this pronouncement, Celia realized what was odd about the Ellsworth women. None of them had put that tawny hair into its usual intricate arrangement. Madeleine's hung down, so you could see how many strands of gray were mixed with the red-brown. Marcia's was twirled in a kind of braid which then dangled to one side. Jill's was held back with a large barrette—rather nice, actually, Celia thought. She noted that the pile of green shavings was larger; some had fallen on Jill's white slacks.

"We ought to tell the manager." Only Cindy looked as usual: the large plump formless face over the green-and-white sweatshirt. "He'll want to call that woman."

"What woman?"

"You remember. She was up here crying, looking for him—what was her name again?"

"Sit down, Cindy," her mother told her sharply. "Just sit."

"Anyhow, this Bernie Lenox, he can give any message himself," Jason pointed out. "If we just wait fifteen minutes."

"What's that?"

"That's when he said he'd be here. He said he'd stop off and then try to get to the hospital before visiting hours were over." If Jason saw Jerry lean over the railing at the sound of a stopping car, he paid no attention.

"The hospital won't let him in," Madeleine said, as if this took care of everything.

"I wouldn't be too sure." Cindy again. "I remember my friend Lois—her grandfather was sick, they said absolutely no visitors. So Lois snuck in anyhow and brought him Chinese food. Not just regular stuff either. The real spicy kind, three dishes in little cardboard containers. And you know what? He ate every bit and got better. He really did. Six months later he was playing golf." She studied their unresponsive faces. Could you get Chinese food around here, she asked.

She knows they're upset, Celia thought. Impossible she should not know. This is her special delight—making it worse, whatever it is. She has them on ice, and why not?

The next second proved her right because Jill brushed the green shavings off her slacks and said—her first comment— "Why don't you shut your mouth?"

"You better not talk to me like that," Cindy said. "Otherwise I'll tell them about that night when you and Marcia—"

Jill slapped her. Palm flat on that blubbery cheek, a shocking noise. Or are all sounds shocking in the country silence, which really is not a silence at all but an amalgam of relaxed harmonious noises. Cindy turned red, then white, and Jill's nose was sharp and white too. In fact, all of them looked sheepish, as if that intemperately raised hand had been a communal offense.

Smoothing things over, Jason leaned forward. "I forgot to tell you how he was coming. This Bernie Lenox. He said a car."

"He never did have a car," Jerry muttered.

"Well, he wouldn't be walking from the bus stop. Almost ten miles." Cindy had recovered fast.

"Maybe that's him now," the male nurse said, as the sound of a car stopping came clearly up to the porch. Excitement is infectious; though Celia had told herself she would remain, a detached observer, a few feet behind them, she found herself leaning over the railing with the rest. A tall thin man carrying golf clubs opened a car door and got out. When Celia moved back, her foot brushed against the pile of shavings.

"That's not him?" Jason turned to the others.

A collective sigh: that was not him.

"Maybe you should tell me what he's like. This man who expects me to smuggle him into Professor Ellsworth's room."

No one answered.

"I gather not tall and thin?"

"He wears this business suit," Cindy said, and giggled. "He writes in a notebook. All kinds of stuff. The population of Vermont. The color of the waitress's eyes. The height of some mountain."

"I see. Pedantic fellow. Well, if someone like that says fifteen minutes—Oh, excuse me." Because the bellboy was beckoning to him again. Celia looked behind, into the Ping-Pong room, when Jason was gone. Dark in there; indeed, since Cindy's friends left, she's never seen anyone actually using the tables. But when the lobby was crowded, or in those intervals before the dining room opened, people did step in there from time to time, sipping drinks, fingering the balls, picking up rackets and giving them experimental little swings. A couple of figures in the darkened room now.

"Flat tire." Jason was back.

"Come again?" Jerry still sounded vaguely truculent.

"That man, Bernie Lenox, he says he got a flat tire. Could hold him up an extra twenty minutes."

"That was Bernie?"

"I just told you."

"Why didn't you let me speak to him?" No attempt at masking the anger now.

"I'd have been glad to," the male nurse said, and brushed a speck off his white jacket. "Next time he calls, if he calls, you'll be the first to know. Besides"—again his deferential little bow—"I figured you'd be seeing him anyhow."

"What the hell does that mean?"

"It's what he said. He wanted to see you before he went on to the hospital."

"Me?" Jerry's sallow face twisted.

"All of you. The whole family. He was very particular about it. He had important business with you, was how he put it."

"Where you going?" A shrill voice, Jill to Marcia, who had moved away.

"Just to get a drink."

"You stay right here." The long fingers were scrabbling at the paint again.

"If you say so." Marcia spoke with that excess of languor that denotes irritation imperfectly concealed, and sat down in a wicker chair. Suddenly Celia thought of the first night

194

she'd seen them. That exuberant group laughing, reaching across the table to say, Here, taste this, giving orders to the waitress and jovially countermanding them. Now they're not just sending out signals of unapproachability to other guests, they're holding each other off.

Even Madeleine had lost the easy imperiousness that comes from being the mastermind of a family. They weren't a family, they were five distinct entities, each looking stubbornly into the night as if unwilling to meet the gaze of anyone else. So when Cindy said, "Maybe not Bernie at all," Celia was the only one to see the mischief working on her face before she spoke.

"Why would someone pretend to be this Bernie?"

"They know he's missing and they think it would be fun to make trouble," Cindy said promptly; one familiar with this kind of inclination.

"Missing!" Jason said. "You told me he was lost—I thought it was a joke. No one said he was really missing."

"Well, he is," Cindy said. "Missing for—how many days is it now?"

No one answered, no one enlightened her, so he asked another question. Missing, what did that mean?

"He didn't get where he was supposed to," Jerry said. "That satisfy you?"

"Maybe a car accident," Jason suggested.

"He took the bus and there were no bus accidents."

"And Marcia and Jill took him to where the bus stops in Anchorville, and they didn't have an accident on the way or we'd know about it," Cindy said with sullen triumph.

Jason spoke quietly. Missing. That made everything different. He didn't know he'd been talking to a man who was missing. Or to someone pretending to be that man. He'd have prolonged the conversation, tried to get a line. . . .

"Pretty dumb," Jerry said.

Jason nodded affably, one willing to accept the blame. He could see: he'd missed the boat. Then his voice sharpened.

He wanted to come back to the earlier question. Besides the trouble-making theory of Cindy's, which sounded plausible but not too plausible, why would someone pretend to be this Bernie Lenox?

During the silence that met this, two more cars drove up. A woman with two boys out of the first one. An elderly couple out of the second. Then Cindy pushed up the sleeves of her sweatshirt. "I get it. Someone killed Bernie and doesn't want us to know."

"Stop talking so dumb." A harsh voice—Celia realized it was Madeleine's. Madeleine going to take charge at last?

"Okay, you suggest something," Cindy said, and when no one did, Jason's conciliating voice spoke again. "Sounds farfetched, I admit. Could be this young lady has been seeing too many movies. On the other hand, stranger things have happened. So let's run with that for a minute. Someone killed him, but they don't want anyone to start looking, they want us to think he's still alive, so they call and say it's him. But they call me because I don't know the voice."

No response, except that Jill got halfway out of her chair and then sat back down.

"It would fit with a grown man being, as you say, missing." Jason gave a speculative smile, pulling at his chin. "So I guess the real question for us, why would someone want to kill Bernie Lenox?"

"He's such a nut," Cindy said with her usual pleased promptitude.

"Oh, Miss."

"Ask anyone. You talk and he writes it down in a notebook. I had this friend up here, Jonathan, Bernie practically didn't know him. But one day he wrote down where Jonathan went to school and what courses and what hotel his parents stayed at when they came to see him. You think I'm kidding? No reason at all, he just does it. So maybe . . ."

Conscious that all eyes were fixed on her, she stood

straight against the railing: Cindy, center stage. "Jonathan wasn't the only one. Hey, Mister—" Because a man in a tweed jacket was walking by: the male half of the bird-watching team. He stopped and looked with courteous puzzlement at the assembled family.

"You knew Bernie, didn't you? Bernie Lenox. Pudgy. The man who was with us. Always wore this business suit."

A nod. Ah, yes. He certainly knew Mr. Lenox.

"Well, listen. We're trying to—I mean, like, did you ever talk to him?"

The man warmed to his subject. Talk? In a manner of speaking, he surely did. He and his wife went bird watching every morning, and when they came back they'd be greeted by those on the porch. How was it? What'd they see? So this one morning, this Mr.—Lenox, did she say? He was on the porch too. Well, everyone always pretends they care a little, common politeness, but what does Mr. Lenox do but write it all down in a little notebook? The name of every species they mention. He hadn't seemed a bird fancier or anything like that, but still, always nice to have someone take an interest.

"Thanks, Mister." Cindy waved him off. "See! What'd I tell you. So—"A furtive look to make sure the man was really gone—"So let's say Bernie wrote down something else, like a name or a time or a date, he didn't know it was important only to this particular person it turned out to be very important."

"Can't you get her to shut up?" Marcia said to her mother.

"So this person, let's call him Mr. X . . ." Another look around, as if for approval of her craftiness. No one gave signs of approving. She shrugged and leaned against the railing. "So this Mr. X, he decides Bernie is a danger through knowing something, he follows him to the bus stop." She turned to Jill. "You guys, did you actually put him on the bus?"

Jill was wearing the black-and-yellow sweater; above it, her features looked sharp and pale. "Put him on?" Her lips barely moved.

"Like, did you wait to see did the bus really come? Or did you just leave him there on the corner?"

A confused mumble. From Marcia, whose tawny hair shines above her hunched-up shoulders? Or from Jill, whose hands are now rigid on the denuded armrests?

"I mean, like, was anyone else standing there, waiting? Someone the police could maybe find and check with?"

"It's too morbid. She shouldn't be allowed."

"I think it's interesting," the male nurse said. "She's a clever kid."

"So that goofy Bernie, let's say he never gets on the bus at all." Cindy sent Jason a blurry smile of thanks: nothing is going to stop her now. "He stands there and a car comes along and it's that Mr. X. Or maybe a woman, how should I know? Mrs. X. Anyhow, they offer him a ride, and he's just dumb enough, the poor nut, Bernie, I mean, he just gets in the car where someone is fixing to kill him, he—"

"Make her stop, make her stop, make her stop. I didn't do it. I didn't. Marcia told me, she was the one, she said—" For a second Celia thought it must go on and on, that shrill wail emerging from the crumpled yellow-and-black mass that was Jill. But someone had a hand on her shoulder.

"All right, Miss, take it easy," Officer Hurley said, and she realized he had been there, in the Ping-Pong room, the whole time.

20

"NOW CAN I KNOW what that was all about?" She and Jason were on the porch. Though people passed from time to time, no one looked at them with any particular curiosity. Hurley had accomplished what he had to with amazing tact: the Ellsworths taken off so almost no one in the hotel knew what was going on. In the view of the couple standing with their drinks a few feet away or the bellboy straightening chairs or the man checking out the sky for a line on tomorrow's weather, it was a night at the Cedar Springs Inn like any other.

"You mean Bernie?" Though he still had on the white pants, Jason had taken off the white jacket; under it was a gray sweater. The male nurse giving way to the professor of literature.

"I mean everything," Celia said.

"Bernie first. You told me, in no special order, a number of things in connection with that man. That poor nut, as Cindy I guess rightly calls him. One, Jill and Marcia were driving him to the bus station. Two, on the day of his departure, Marcia had bought a large size man's shirt and slacks of the cheapest possible variety. Three, to account for the extra hundred and eighty miles on the car and the huge stink of whiskey on the back seat, Jill and Marcia gave their sister some preposterous explanation about a high old night in the bars with two men they'd picked up. And four, a woman who worked with Bernie reported that though noted as a punctilious man, he didn't arrive home on schedule. So once I knew someone was being very diabolical—"

"That's really what I—"

"Celia, let's get Bernie out of the way first. Once I was not just hearing chatter about the Ellsworths but listening for intimations of trouble, I did in fact see how out of those four relatively innocuous circumstances a ghoulish scenario could be discerned. But how to prove it? How in God's name to prove it? So Hurley—very reasonable fellow, your local police boss—Hurley said okay; on the chance that someone might break down, I could play around with a little gimmick of my own. Possible, of course, only if they had no idea I was anything except a dumb and also disinterested onlooker. Which was why"—a lowered voice, a brief smile—"I couldn't recognize you. I had to be the nurse and only that."

"Male nurse," she murmured.

"A bow to Cindy. Yes. A double bow because what I didn't expect was all the cooperation I would get from her. That unfortunate girl who's too young, evidently, to have been taken into the family confidence but old enough to perceive when there's a chance to work up family embarrassment."

"That's how she gets her kicks. Turning the screw."

"In this case, I have to thank her." Jason folded the white coat and laid it across the railing. "That business of Bernie calling me up, Bernie threatening to come, Bernie and his flat tire—Jill was squirming, but like the others she's a cool customer; I don't know that she'd have cracked. But with Cindy unwittingly setting the stage, Bernie in a car with a woman who had reason to kill him . . ."

"So Marcia and Jill really . . . I should have guessed. Of course. Long ago he really was married to Marcia; he must have been in on the family secret."

A long sidelong glance from Jason. Did she by any chance know that secret too?

But she shook her head. "For the moment, let's stick to Bernie."

"Well, it turns out Cindy was right. He never did get on that bus. Their scheme was not too bad. Shoot this man who was unattached, whom no one would put up a concerted search for, dress him in some cheap nondescript clothing with I assume all identification removed, pour whiskey over him to make him reek like a wino, and dump him someplace where winos are a dime a dozen. Even winos with a bullet wound in the chest. Well, it happens Albany is ninety miles from Cedar Springs, and also—Hurley came across with this—Jill once worked there in some topless restaurant: she knew the terrain. Anyhow, when Hurley called the Albany police it turned out that on one of those unspeakable streets where a dead bum doesn't make any headlines, there had been someone answering Bernie's description. By tomorrow, unless the police of some other city put out an alert for him, which our friends knew was not likely to happen, the medical examiner's office down there would have released him to be buried in whatever grave they reserve for unclaimed bums."

"And that poor woman would have gone on forever thinking he'd run out on her. Just decided to skip out on everything." Celia closed her eyes. She had stood right here, Bernie's friend, carrying all the appurtenances of the born loser. The bad teeth. The splotchy skin. The pinched features. The inappropriate navy dress, mate to Bernie's inappropriate suit. And of course that vulnerable story with its dual components: one, that the hardware store was a losing proposition, and two, that Bernie had told her a windfall from some unspecified source was in the works. "Man with money in his pocket, lots of times they go getting ideas," Jill had meanly said, her face glittering under the splendid hair. But it was the Ellsworths who got the ideas:

how to get rid of a poor nut who deluded himself that he could blackmail them and make it work.

"So that's why there was that smell of whiskey in the car."

Jason nodded. That was why.

"They just dumped him and left him?"

"Looks like it. Or at least it will look like it, I suspect, when some official from Cedar Springs gets to examine that body in Albany."

She looked out at the spacious night scene. Still heavy clouds, but here and there the heartening glimpse of stars; tomorrow just might be fine. "Jason, how did you know to come up here?"

"God, it seems years ago—only ten o'clock this morning? Actually, Ellsworth asked me."

She stared at him.

"In a manner of speaking, he asked me. Celia, remember his last dictation—you played me the tape. Such a pleasure for him to have his daughter-in-law and Jerry, the extra indulgences, unaccustomed treats, plus two added sets of discerning ears . . . Don't wince. He knew what he was doing, that canny operator. And after that paean to family caretakers, a look at Maisie. Henry James's Maisie. Poor unfortunate Maisie, betrayed by all four parents and at last taken in tow by the governess whose only wish is for the child to be happy. That's what the tape said. Happy. And like an idiot I didn't really listen, or at any rate I didn't absorb it. You were sort of upset—"

"You can say it. Hysterical."

Jason ran his hand over the flowers. "Anyhow, you blew your top, and that put everything else out of my mind. Till this morning. That phone call when you said you couldn't get in, they wouldn't let you in. Celia, you must be a wreck. Can I get you a drink? Something from the kitchen?"

"Just keep talking."

"So that phone call—something clicked. I replayed that tape in my head: Henry James with a governess who wants her little charge to be happy. Jesus. Because the truth is of course that Mrs. Wix couldn't care less whether Maisie is happy or not. On that last dreadful day, when the child has gotten the bad news from Sir Claude over chocolate and rolls, Mrs. Wix has only one question: Has the moral sense stayed intact? It's the question any other responsible person would ask; for those who passed judgment on the child in eighteen ninety-eight, the only question. Celia, not even a sandwich? So then, goodness or badness? Innocence or depravity—in Henry James's mind, in the mind of every authority, the old dichotomy still exists. It may be making its last stand, but it still is going strong. For all the new tolerances, the scientific scrutiny, the mitigating phrases about fun and freedom, childhood at the turn of the century remained a time of basic choice: will the child end up good or bad? Or as Mrs. Wix memorably puts it, Will the moral sense stay intact?

"Hey, Celia, I didn't mean to give a lecture." Jason looked up at the ceiling, where the insects hurled themselves against the overhead lights. "Actually, I did mean. Because the point is, this is the lecture Ellsworth would've given if he'd been free. The only one compatible with what he'd been talking about till now. So this morning, as I say, I thought of it. His giving a diametrically opposite interpretation from the expected one. And then it hit me. It was his way of telling you that everything else he said that morning was the opposite of the truth."

"The lit professor going in for code."

"Exactly."

"Then those two sets of discerning ears for inspiration, one's own family taking care, geared for the extra indulgences, all that about how it set him up . . ."

"You got it," Jason said.

"But why a code at all? Why didn't he just blurt it out? Get them out of here!"

"I asked him that this afternoon. He said they threatened you, said something would happen to you, if he let anything slip."

"Jason . . ."

"Yeah. So now do you get the picture? There he sits, helpless, with those two rotters in charge. So what can he do about it? He can make like an English professor, that's what. Give a phony rendition of a book, and trust you to catch on that his account of his family is similarly phony."

"And dumb me, I missed it. There I was, thinking—"

"I thought it too. Until, as I say, this morning. Then I realized someone had better get there fast. But get there how? In what shape? A friend, someone vaguely suspect, wouldn't have a chance. They'd give him the boot the way they gave it to you. But if it could be someone anonymous, some nonentity with no reason to be interested. Then I remembered. Fellow on the floor below me was a nurse."

She pictured him standing at that front door, making his inexorable way past a blustering Jerry. "Jason, is there such a thing as the Association of Male Nurses, Eastern Division?"

"Sounds convincing, doesn't it?" He did allow himself a self-congratulatory smile. Well, he rates it.

Then something else. "That fire, which got Les out of the way. Did they set it?"

He leaned back in the wicker chair Jill had denuded. "Could be. Hurley says he's looking into it. Like that dead body in Albany, still a lot of details that need to be looked into."

"Jason, those two. Rotters, you called them. Did they hurt him in any way?"

"You mean, did they beat him? Deprive him of his medicine? Refuse to close the window when he felt a draft? No. All they did was keep him incommunicado when he wanted to call his lawyer. You know the way he was set up, no phone in his room. For him to make a call, someone had to bring a phone, attach it to a jack in the wall."

"They wouldn't?"

"Wouldn't let him get any message out. Actually, that was the main reason to go to the hospital. Not to have treatment for his ailing heart but to ensure privacy for his vital business."

"What business was that?"

"I'm not sure I have it straight. Once I'd done my part, I was out of it. I think maybe Officer Hurley had better tell you. Hurley and that lawyer."

"So a lawyer did come."

"Lawyer, accountants, bank officers, custodian of funds, notary—a whole world of finance has been congregated in that hospital room this afternoon. Celia, I think that's the lawyer now."

She looked down to the curb. A wiry gray-haired man getting out of a car, Hurley behind him. The man walked slowly—big afternoon, as Jason said—but his handshake was firm and his eyes rested with gratification on Celia. "So this is the young lady we have to thank."

"Me! I didn't even—"

"It's the way my client reported it. Due to the perspicacity of Celia Sommerville."

"Listen. I'd have muffed it. I mean, if not for Jason . . ."

"Well, let's say you and he were a very effective combine. Incidentally, I should introduce myself. Curt Menaker."

She said she was glad to meet him.

"I'm glad I could be here, I'll tell you that. From what I've been gathering, it was far from being a sure thing."

Jason pointed out that Celia still didn't understand the urgency.

"You didn't tell her what we did?"

"I thought you should," Jason demurred.

When Mr. Menaker turned, light shone on the wavy gray

hair, the grave eyes, the tired mouth. But nothing tired about his voice as it rolled out over the quiet porch. "Fact is, my dear friend Eric Ellsworth turned over all his financial assets to his university. The bulk of it to go for a new library and the rest for various fellowships." He paused, but only to wait for Hurley to give orders to an assistant. "A fairly complicated business. Several times I doubted that in the course of an afternoon it could be accomplished. But if everyone is willing at a moment's notice to ride in small private aircraft and come down on pocket-size landing fields and in general move with a lot more alacrity than they feel comfortable doing . . ." He looked out at the sky, where the clouds were beginning to disperse. "Why do I sound surprised? It's always been my experience that for money of that dimension, people are willing to put themselves out to a very considerable degree." Then his gaze turned from the view, he looked again at Celia. "I should add that the addendum about Celia Sommerville's perspicacity accompanies the gift. Your stock at the university, my dear, is going to be very high."

"I could use a little of that," she said.

"She deserves a little of that," Jason said, and gave her another of the long looks.

"Well, she has it," Mr. Menaker said. "At one point there was even talk of a Sommerville fellowship—No, don't worry, I said you wouldn't. But plenty of people will appreciate . . ." The sonorous voice trailed off; there was a hushed air about the three men as they all turned toward the darkness beyond the porch. Something self-consciously solemn, rigid, respectful.

She looked from one to another. "Is there something you're not telling me?"

"Look here, my dear," Mr. Menaker said. "It was a lot of excitement for a sick, elderly man. Twice during the afternoon his doctor came in and suggested that the proceedings be postponed. So he was fully aware of the risks."

206

"He's dead, isn't he?"

"Out of his misery," Hurley said piously. "Died in peace."

"He wanted to finish that book . . ." Who would believe it? On a hotel porch, Celia Sommerville crying for a man she's known for only nine days.

"He liked doing it. He told me that. You were a great help to him."

"I did nothing. I just switched on that damn machine. I didn't even have the sense to realize . . . after all those eloquent explanations . . ."

"Well, he had the chance, at the end, to order things exactly the way he wanted. Not every man can say that."

This is his eulogy; this and the ensuing stillness broken only by the hum of crickets, a dog barking, the rumble of distant thunder. The stillness a troubled man chose to live with for his last years. Then Hurley with a little click of heels reminded the meeting that there was still business up for discussion. "I'm not knocking you lawyers and accountants and credit officers and what not," he said. "But what beats me—a sick man who knew he had only a short time to live—why all that elaborate folderol? If he wanted a university and not the family to get his money, why didn't he just change his will?"

A different silence this time, one broken by throat clearings, coughing, averted glances, superfluous shrugs of shoulder. "I think I know," Celia finally said.

"I sure wish you'd explain the financial gimmicks."

"Nothing to do with finance." When she looked around, Mr. Menaker's gaze met hers in quiet complicity. "Did he tell you?" she asked.

"Just before he died. The irony is, that's all that was on his mind when he first wanted me called. He just felt this great need to unburden himself. I suppose he'd been giving signals of this, and that was what alerted them." Mr. Menaker looked inquiringly at her and she nodded. Signals to me too: *Authors are lucky; in position, as we humans are not, to dole out whatever punishments they think are due.*

Mr. Menaker rubbed his eyes; a man who'd put in a long day. "And had they let me come, Madeleine and the son, that would have been the end of it. A talk of the utmost confidentiality between attorney and client. But they were afraid, those two miserable creatures. They didn't know what complications might come of it."

"They were always afraid," she said. "Afraid of letting him have a visit from Lee Elliott. Afraid of letting them hear about George's death. Afraid of anything that might trigger that troubled mind into a precipitate confession. And I don't know. In their terms, maybe they were right, maybe they were."

"Well, they finally outsmarted themselves," Menaker said. "They put on that sadistic performance, an old man kept a prisoner, and at last it tipped him off. He knew what kind of people they really were."

"They wouldn't let a minister in either," she said. "He must have tried him before he asked for you."

"So he wanted a minister, Ellsworth did." Melancholy was inscribed on the long grave face. "Maybe it's universal—that need for absolution when people feel themselves nearing the end." Then the gravity was touched by wonder. "My dear, did he tell you too?"

"No." She paused. How explain to them that moment when she stood in the tangle of wet shrubbery and suddenly it all came together?

Down at the curb, a car stopped; a man and woman got out and started an agitated conversation. Their voices were unintelligible, but her mind played out the words. Looks all right, let's go in—what the woman is saying? They probably charge a mint—her husband? Six hours on the road, I sure as hell could use a bed and bath. Snazzy place like that, they probably have no vacancy anyhow.

Is that how the other three hear it? She felt them looking at her. "No one told me anything. I just . . . I mean . . ."

"Maybe we're not talking about the same thing," Mr. Menaker said.

"I think we are," she said firmly. "Does it include a ten-year-old boy who looks out a window of his bedroom and in the driveway below sees something he's not supposed to see?"

Hurley suddenly hit the side of the railing: not the small-town philosopher at all. "Now look here. It's eleven o'clock. I arrested people I thought were decent folk, I escorted half a dozen bigwigs from airplanes, I spent more time than is my preference guarding a hospital corridor. And I saw a good man die. A man—I'm not ashamed to say it—I learned to love. So would you two stop pussyfooting around so I can go home to bed?"

Mr. Menaker tore off one of the geraniums. "I loved him too. I still love him."

"For Christ's sake, man, out with it." Jason, also at the end of his rope.

"I may have had more difficult statements to make in my life, but if so I don't remember. Well, here goes." But even now he didn't immediately go; he took time to sigh and modulate his voice, so only the three of them could hear its deep clear syllables. "So, Eric Ellsworth, my good friend who was married to a woman not worthy of him. No one has ever been in any doubt about what kind of woman Suzanne was. The succession of men. The drinking. The deceit. Or worse still, the assumption after a while that no deceit was necessary, she was in position to brazen it out. So what does a husband do? A man of great sensitivity. How does he handle this kind of conduct? First he deludes himself that the conduct doesn't exist, and then he tries to change it, and then, sick at heart, he realizes he will have to put up with it."

Celia stared at Mr. Menaker. He's still evading. Can't bring himself to say it.

"Except there comes a time when the inner hurt is so intense, his judgment is affected. He's no longer capable of weighing, assessing. Morality gets dimmed by pain." Mr. Menaker turned from the flowers—he might have been the one in pain. "I know the accepted theory. Suzanne was drinking and got into a car and went over a cliff. Till a couple of hours ago it was my theory."

"My God." Hurley? Jason? She didn't take her eyes from Mr. Menaker.

"That's it. She was dead when he put her into that car and drove in the rain to that cliff, what's its name?"

"Eagle Rock." Hurley, struggling to accept the unacceptable. "He told you all this? It's not guesswork?"

Oh, Officer Hurley, how you're prepared to disparage guesswork, turn your practiced contempt on it. And how this time you wish that guesswork was what you had to deal with.

"He told me. It's also, I assume, what he wanted to tell that minister. He drove her in the car, then got out just at the strategic moment, then—well, you don't need the details."

"But what I don't understand"—Hurley's face was twisted—"why didn't he just divorce her?"

"He could have. God knows he had grounds. Another man would have. But Ellsworth was—"

"Ah, yes. Proud," Hurley said.

The two men looked at each other. "A proud fool. He'd divorced his first wife for the same reason. He couldn't say, this man whose distinguished reputation was his dear possession, that he'd done it again, made exactly the same mistake the second time around. Picked another lemon. He couldn't expose himself to the derision he imagined this would cause. So in a deranged moment, he took the other course." Mr. Menaker wiped his forehead. "And that's it. The whole story."

Celia looked down at the lawn, but what she saw was an old man lying under a plaid blanket. An old tormented man who turned to literature in the mistaken hope that it would help him. "What makes children act the way they do," he'd asked the first time they met. Well, about his own children—grandchildren—he knew, or thought he knew. "However they turn out, best to remember you have a part in it"—something else he had said. His credo, you might say. It was why he would put up with them: the shabby lives, the transparent fabrications. Not just put up with them: avert his eyes from the shabbiness and add some corroborating details of his own to the fabrications. *Best to remember*—he remembered all right, lying there day after day.

"Well, it's not quite the whole story," she said. "There's still that ten-year-old boy who was looking out his bedroom window when his father was carrying out the dead woman. The father he had until then adored."

A sizzling noise, but just another maddened insect, scorching itself against the light. "Didn't make much difference for a few years. At least I don't know if it made a difference. But at fifteen, sixteen, seventeen, that age when any traumas get exacerbated." That's her voice, taking over, holding the three of them. "He wouldn't talk to his father, wouldn't see him, wouldn't visit him on vacations. For one eighteen-month period, he didn't go home. Don't ask me how he managed, a sixteen-year-old kid on his own. And of course no one could figure what was going on; who in a prep school is going to guess that the reason a boy throws back his father's presents is because the man killed his wife." She paused; a bellboy came out to look them over, these people who are having themselves a time on the porch at an hour when most guests have gone to their rooms.

"Except one person at the school did know. Roy told his roommate. George always knew."

"I still don't see—" Jason began, but it was Hurley she was looking at. "If you kill someone you don't inherit their money. You're the one who tipped me to it."

Hurley gave his short inexpressive nod, but his lips stayed closed. He's not going to help her out. It's still her party. All right, keep going. "If the truth would be out—well, you all know this better than I do—if anyone came clean, the one to get Suzanne's money would be the nearest relative. That's Lee Elliott. Suzanne's cousin. No, her cousin's son. Roy knew this, his wife did, his three oldest children did. And somewhere along the way, that poor simp Bernie found out."

"And George?" Jason suggested.

"Of course George. That was why he went to see Lee Elliott. Not to buy a table but to check on a man's existence." A thorough man, George. Thorough even when preparing to embark on blackmail.

"So now do you get it?" Mr. Menaker said. "Why Ellsworth did it this way? A deed of gift, which is not a hundred percent foolproof, maybe, but as good as you can get. He wanted to make sure the money was disposed of, safe in the hands he had designated, in case any of this came out."

Hurley said slowly he got it.

Does this wind it up? No, not quite. "That money we're talking about," she said. "It gave the professor no pleasure, just the opposite. Well, look at the way he lived, never touching a penny of it. And it bothered Roy even more. I mean, from the evidence it must have. Even when he was married and sort of reconciled to his father, it bugged him. Lee Elliott, the rightful heir of Suzanne's millions. So when Lee needed money to get set up in business, that was Roy's big chance. A hundred thousand dollars. Then another hundred thousand, even though he couldn't afford it. Poor miserable man, I just hope it made him feel good."

Another pause while they all absorbed this. Then Mr. Menaker cleared his throat. He congratulated her, he nicely said. In nine days—was it only nine—to have found all this out.

"Actually, something I'd like to find out. Which of them killed George?"

"You don't have to wonder about that." What a relief for Hurley: authoritative at last. "By now they're in the stage of each blabbing on the other, trying to save their own skin. Jerry did it, that time he was supposed to be eating chocolate bars on a mountain."

"Well, if Jerry killed George and Marcia and Jill rang the bell on Bernie"—she closed her eyes for a second, but there it was, the large, masterful face with its facile theatrics bearing down on her—"does that mean the mother goes scot free?"

"I know what you're thinking," Hurley said. "Don't worry, Miss Sommerville. We have her for conspiracy. The one thing they all agree on is they were following Mama's orders. Besides, she's the one who kept the professor a prisoner—I wouldn't be surprised if there's a case to be made that it's this treatment that brought on the fatal heart attack."

Surely finished now—dimly she heard Mr. Menaker. The management of this very pleasant hotel had promised to hold a room for him, he figured it was about time to claim it.

After a pat on her shoulder that she realized was meant to be congratulatory, Hurley went with him; she and Jason were alone on the porch.

"Not exactly finished for everyone." And when he looked at her, "I was thinking of Cindy," she said. "That mixed up, blubbery, disagreeable girl—to find out her

213

mother and brother and two sisters have been ticketed as murderers."

"And her grandfather," Jason said. "Her distinguished, erudite grandfather, whose action started it all." What a situation for a young girl, he added when his voice was under control. The worst. But two strangers, what could he and Celia do?

"We're at a university, and since our reputation there, as Mr. Menaker says, is going to be on the high side . . ."

"Your reputation."

"Both," she said firmly. "You heard what he said. A combine." Down on the lawn, she saw, the lights that shone on the sign were being dimmed. The Cedar Springs Inn was not interested in transients who came looking for rooms at this hour. "Anyhow, assuming the girl's record is halfway decent, if we could get her admitted and then sort of keep an eye on her."

"You really think—"

"We could try. Especially because we don't like her, I think we sort of have to try. I mean, this might just be a case where it really is important that the moral sense stays intact."

When Jason moved, she could see the geraniums glistening—each one upright, hopeful, waiting to receive the dew of another day.

"Agreed," Jason said. "Just so it's understood Cindy won't be the only project this combine will be involved in."